Robert Jephson

Julia - Or the Italian lover - A Tragedy

As it is Acted at the Theatre-Royal, in Drury-Lane

Robert Jephson

Julia - Or the Italian lover - A Tragedy
As it is Acted at the Theatre-Royal, in Drury-Lane

ISBN/EAN: 9783337038854

Printed in Europe, USA, Canada, Australia, Japan

Cover: Foto ©Andreas Hilbeck / pixelio.de

More available books at **www.hansebooks.com**

J U L I A:

OR, THE

I T A L I A N   L O V E R.

A

T R A G E D Y.

AS IT IS ACTED AT THE

T H E A T R E-R O Y A L,

IN

D R U R Y-L A N E.

By ROBERT JEPHSON, Esq.

—primus amor deceptam morte fefellit. VIRG.

D U B L I N:

Printed for Messrs. W. WATSON, CHAMBERLAINE,
MONCRIEFFE, COLLES, BURNET, WILKINSON,
WHITE, GILBERT. BYRNE, WOGAN, SLEATER,
H. WHITSTONE, WALKER, COLBERT, JONES,
PARKER, BURTON, LEWIS, M'KENZIE, MOORE,
DORNIN, HALPEN, and COONEY.

MDCCLXXXVIII.

TO

HIS GRACE

CHARLES DUKE OF RUTLAND,

KNIGHT OF THE MOST NOBLE ORDER OF THE
GARTER,

LORD LIEUTENANT OF IRELAND,

&c. &c. &c.

IN TESTIMONY OF

UNALTERABLE ESTEEM,

AFFECTION, AND GRATITUDE,

THIS TRAGEDY IS INSCRIBED,

BY HIS GRACE'S MUCH OBLIGED,

AND MOST OBEDIENT,

HUMBLE SERVANT,

Dublin Castle,
April 11, 1787.

ROBERT JEPHSON.

PERSONS REPRESENTED.

Duke of Genoa,	Mr. PACKER.
Durazzo, *a Nobleman, father of* Julia,	Mr. BENSLEY.
Mentevole, *a young Nobleman, in love with* Julia,	Mr. KEMBLE.
Marcellus, *a young Nobleman, son of* Fulvia,	Mr. PALMER.
Camillo, *his cousin and friend,*	Mr. WHITFIELD.
Manoa, *a Merchant,*	Mr. AIKIN.
Fulvia, *mother of* Marcellus,	Mrs. WARD.
Julia, *daughter of* Durazzo,	Mrs. SIDDONS.
Olympia, *her friend, and sister of* Mentevole,	Mrs. BRERETON.
Nerina, *attendant on* Julia,	Miss TIDSWELL.

Officer, Guards, and Attendants.

S C E N E, Genoa.

J U L I A:

OR,

THE ITALIAN LOVER.

A

T R A G E D Y.

ACT I. SCENE I.

A Platform.

Enter MARCELLUS, *supporting* MANOA ; *Attendants be-bind.*

MARCELLUS.

LOOK up, Sir ; you are safe. The tempest's wild-
nefs
Seems hufh'd on fhore.   Where was your veffel bound ?

MANOA.

Ancona was her port ; the hurricane
Baffled our pilot's fkill, and drove us headlong
(Juft as your fhip made good her anchorage,)
On the fharp rock, where you beheld her fplit.
All my companions, fifty lucklefs men,
Sunk in my fight ; and I had fhar'd their fate,
Had not your ftrong arm fav'd me.   But, alas,
We are in Genoa, if mine eyes deceive not.

B

MARCELLUS.

The fame.

MANOA.

Too well I know it.   Shield me Heaven!
For what am I referv'd?

MARCELLUS.

I hope, to lofe
The memory of your grief, and find peace here.

MANOA.

O no! to lofe my life, if I'm found here.

MARCELLUS.

Pray, let me know your ftory.   By your habit
'guefs you are not of our faith or nation.

MANOA.

I am by birth of Syria; but here fojourn'd
Twice twenty years in wealth and fair repute,
'Till Chriftian malice, or my nation's curfe,
Or both combining, turn'd me forth a wanderer.
Look there, that very manfion once was mine.

MARCELLUS.

I now recall fome traces of that face;
Your name is Manoa?

MANOA.

Ay, that wretch am I.
Thou haft an afpect fo benign and noble,
Thou could'ft not injure me.

MARCELLUS.

Myfelf much fooner.

MANOA.

This ftate, for its late levies 'gainft the Tuik,
Call'd on all traffickers for fums of gold;
Our tribe, at my perfuafion, furnifh'd them,
On rates fo eafy to the borrowers,
The native merchants' offers were refus'd,
And publick clamour, and difgrace, purfued them:
Thence grew their hate. Of black and monftrous crimes
Avouch'd on oath by witneffes fuborn'd,
They charg'd me guiltlefs; flight alone was left,
To fave my hunted life.

MARCELLUS.

MARCELLUS.

And I remember,
'Twas rumour'd you had perish'd by the sea,
Attempting your escape ; and so believ'd :
Knaves call'd your fate a judgment.

MANOA.

To prevent
A hot pursuit, the Hebrews here in Genoa
By common concert spread abroad that rumour.
The death they feign'd, this morning, but for thee,
My brave preserver, had indeed o'erta'en me.

MARCELLUS.

I can do more to serve you. Name your wish.

MANOA.

At present, this. Not far from hence resides
The lord Durazzo, whose great wealth and power,
As heaven sends dews and sunshine, are dispens'd
To gladden every humble thing beneath them.
Let your men help me there, for I am feeble ;
And this disguise may save me from the note
Of those who pass,—though in this slothful city
Few leave their down so early.

MARCELLUS.

Sir, farewel !
You shall hear more of me.

MANOA

Accept my prayers !
My heart's too full to speak the thanks I owe you.
[*Exit* MANOA, *with Attendants.*

MARCELLUS.

He has been sorely wrong'd.—But who goes there ?
[CAMILLO *passes over the stage.*
I cannot sure mistake him : 'Tis Camillo.
Good kinsman, turn, and own a friend who loves you.
CAMILLO *returns.*

S C E N E II.

CAMILLO, MARCELLUS.

CAMILLO.

A gentle invitation. Ha! Marcellus!
Welcome once more to Genoa, my dear cousin.
                              [*embracing.*
We heard you had escap'd with some slight hurts
That bloody lingering business there at Candia ;
But such fierce storms of late have swept our coasts,
Our fears were, lest the angry elements,
Leaguing alike against the Christian cross,
Might prove worse woes even than the infidels.

MARCELLUS.

We had rough weather, but our sturdy bark
Out-rode it. Is my mother well ? At leisure
I shall fatigue your ear with other questions
My ignorance and your kindness must excuse.

CAMILLO.

You have not seen her then ?

MARCELLUS.

                    No I arriv'd
Within this hour ; and knowing how she lov'd.
Lov'd even to dotage, my poor brother Claudio,
(Lost by a fate so strange and horrible,)
I would not rush at once into her presence,
Till some kind friend, like you, should first inform me,
How best to assuage her grief, and hide my own.

CAMILLO.

Thought like a son. But O, his vanish'd form,
Again presented in your living likeness,
Will with the strong extreme convulse her soul,
And joy so mix'd with anguish doubly shake her.

MARCELLUS.

'Twas what I fear'd, Camillo. I must try then
To fix her fond attention on myself,
And shun that direful theme.

                              CAMILLO.

CAMILLO.

　　　　　　Direful indeed!
(How my heart shrinks even now to think of it!)
'Tis ever present to her tortur'd fancy:
And we who daily see her, have obferv'd,
Our care to give the current of her thoughts
A different courfe, but fwells up her impatience.
You know the lady Fulvia's ardent temper,
How fudden, yet how ftrong in every feeling.

MARCELLUS.

Our burning mountains, when their fires burft forth,
Rage not more fiercely than her breaft Inflam'd.
But is it poffible, in all this time,
Months after months elaps'd, no light, no fpark,
To guide to a difcovery has been trac'd?
The Turkifh gallies fo o'erfpread the fea,
My letters rarely reach'd me while at Candia.

CAMILLO.

What have you heard?

MARCELLUS.

　　　　　But thus much, and no more:
Two days ere that for his intended marriage
With good Durazzo's daughter, lovely Julia,
Was Claudio miffing; two days more were pafs'd
In fruitlefs fearch, and fad anxiety:
When on the fifth, fome weary mariners,
Flying for fhelter from a furious ftorm,
Midft the white caverns on the weftern fhore,
A mile from Genoa, found his lifelefs body:
In his clench'd hand was his own blood-ftain'd fword,
And in his manly breaft a mortal wound.

CAMILLO.

And there ends all our knowledge.　Proclamation
Of vaft rewards to find his murderer,
Is ftill abroad through all the Italian ftates.
The untouch'd jewels of his coftly habit,
Bright and confpicuous, clearly manifeft
'Twas not the crime of men who kill for fpoil.

　　　　　　　　MAR-

MARCELLUS.

Alas, Camillo, well I know the place ;
When we were boys it was our favourite haunt.
He could not sure have fall'n by his own sword ?

CAMILLO.

Impoſſible : A thought ſo black and ſullen
Ne'er dim'd the ſunſhine of his chearful breaſt:
The joy he long had ſigh'd for in his reach,
Poſſeſs'd of all that gilds the morn of life,
And each fair proſpect bright'ning to his hopes ;
Beſides, the exalted tenour of his mind,
Too firm and fu'l for wild extremities ;
They cruſh that black concluſion: nay the ſkilful,
Who ſearch'd the wound with cloſeſt art and care,
Pronounc'd it not the execrable work
Of his own ſword, but ſome aſſaſſin's ſteel.

MARCELLUS.

May wakeful conſcience, like a writhing ſnake,
If ſtill he lives, curl round the villain's heart,
With ſharpeſt venom to conſume and gnaw him !
I know our baſe, Italian, ſtabbing ſpirit ;
In the cloſe art of ſpirit none excell us.
We tread the very earth, breathe the ſame air,
With our old Latin ſires ; but, for their virtues,
As well might eagles ruſtle their large plumes
Where owlets rooſt, or filthy kites engender,
As they find ſhelter in our daſtard breaſts.

CAMILLO.

Let others rail ; but thine's a nobler taſk ;
To ſhame degen'racy by fair example ;
For twenty forward ſpirits, like thine own,
Might ſhake this ſtate from its inglorious trance,
And rouſe our ſloth to gallant enterpriſe.

MARCELLUS.

I left it a luxurious, worthleſs city,
Proud of its traſh, its wealth ; if ſuch I find it,
I will not ſtrike my lazy root at home,
To rot in rank contagious apathy,
But ſeek again a ſcene of vigorous action.

The

The unfkilful perfeverance of the Turk
Still wakes excitement for a foldier's ardour.——
But who are thofe fo earneft in difcourfe ?
This way they move.

CAMILLO.

Durazzo is the eldeft.

MARCELLUS.

Fair Julia's father ; him I know. The other?

CAMILLO.

Mentevole his name, a noble youth,
And fuitor (hopelefsly, I think,) to Julia,
Though vulgar fame calls him a favour'd wooer.
But this report, ftartling your mother's ear,
(Who brooks no flight to her fon's memory,)
Has much eftrang'd her from Durazzo's houfe :
And thus, the bonds of their long amity
The lie with many mouths has puff'd afunder.

MARCELLUS.

My care fhall be to reunite their friendfhip.
But how muft I efteem Mentevole ?

CAMILLO.

As one accomplifh'd, brave, and liberal.
Soon after your departure for the fiege,
He came from travel home, and was to Claudio
A fecond felf.

MARCELLUS.

So fhall he be to me ;
I'll wear him here. But go thou to my mother,
Prepare her for my coming. For a moment
Leave me to greet this venerable lord,
And beg his introduction to the ftranger. [*Exit* CAM.

S C E N E III.

To MARCELLUS, DURAZZO, *and* MENTEVOLE.

The ruddy hue your vifage owns, my lord,
I fee with pleafure is found health's true enfign :
Your eye's quick fpirit too, proclaims you frefh
As when the race of carelefs youth began.

DURAZZO.

DURAZZO.

Such is your wish, Marcellus, and I thank you.
O welcome, to thy country ! thy smooth cheek
Has chang'd its down for manhood since we parted.
But for these well-known kindred lineaments,
I scarce durst swear, thou wert that playful boy,
Whose frolicks used to mar our gravity,
And make us smile while chiding.

MARCELLUS.

I remember
Your goodness always ; now entreat your favour,
To recommend me to this lord's esteem,
As, by the title of my brother's friend,
He claims already mine.

DURAZZO.

Mentevole,
Give him your hand.

MENTEVOLE.

My heart too, 'twas his brother's ;
And by that pledge grows thus at once acquainted.

DURAZZO.

Marcellus, you must tell me of your wars,
Your mines, your follies, ambuscades, and dangers.
Though now 'tis long since I was cased in steel,
The crescent of our swarthy foe has felt me.

MARCELLUS.

They are sluggish soldiers, but right obstinate :
So numerous too, it seems an easier task
To kill, than count them.   Now twice fifty thousand,
And more, have fall'n, in sacking one poor isle ;
Yet like light foam chaf'd by the curling surge,
Each hour new turbans whiten round its shores.—
But yet I have not visited my mother,
And she by this expects me.

DURAZZO.

Get thee to her.
Unhappy lady, may your presence cheer her !
[*Exit* MARCELLUS.

SCENE

SCENE IV.

DURAZZO, MENTEVOLE.

Is he not like to Claudio?

MENTEVOLE.

Rather fay,
Is't not himfelf, as ere the tomb received him?
But dear my lord, by all that charm'd your youth,
Forgive me, though I feem importunate:
O, win your daughter to accept my vows;
For I have lov'd to fuch a mad excefs,
So ftor'd up every thought of happinefs
In that fond hope, fhould I prove bankrupt there,
I dare not look to earth or Heaven for comfort.

DURAZZO.

Mentevole, I doubt not of your love;
My daughter too believes it; a feign'd paffion
Speakes not your fervent language:—

MENTEVOLE.

A feign'd paffion!
Thus hear me fwear—

DURAZZO.

Oaths are unneceffary.
My tongue has not been niggard of your praife;
I've tried entreaties too. A harfh command,
Heard with repugnancy, that fhe fhould love,
Becaufe her anxious father deems it meet,
Or you would have it fo, might change at once
The difference you complain of to averfion.
Thus the calm leak that flept at peace before,
Turns a ftrong tide, and fets againft your wifhes.

MENTEVOLE.

O, the degrees, my lord, are infinite,
Between a harfh command, and fuch perfuafion
As every day the fondeft parents ufe,
In tender ftrife with a coy maid's reluctance.
Were I to plead as a feed advocate,
Even for a fcanty rood of barren earth,
I fhould account me faithlefs to my charge,
My rhetorick o'erpriz'd at one poor ducat,

Did

Did I neglect a glofs, or argument,
Might fway the unwilling judge to my decifion.

DURAZZO.
Inftruct me to fpeed better. I fhall thank you.

MENTEVOLE.
My words, my action, fhould have life and grace ;
I'd probe his reafon, try his every humour,
Wind to his inmoft foul, grow to his eye,
Watch where impreffion ftole upon his fenfe ;
There ply my ftrength, where moft I found him weak,
Nor ceafe to urge till I had conquer'd him.

DURAZZO.
Paffion thus blindfolded fees no obftacle.
Young man, young man, be calm a while, and hear me.

MENTEVOLE.
Yet tell me not, my fuit is defperate ;
Sooth, though you cannot heal ; and I will liften,
As if I liv'd by every found you utter'd,
And death and inattention were the fame.

DURAZZO.
You knew long fince, to fee my daughter wedded,
Without a variance 'twixt her choice and mine,
Was my prime wifh. Malignant deftiny
Marr'd that fair profpect. The affaffin's ftab
Had almoft pierc'd with one pernicious ftroke
Two faithful breafts. Anguifh unutterable
On her foft frame lay'd fuch a deadly grafp,
Too long I trembled for her life and reafon.

MENTEVOLE.
Spare me, my lord, O fpare me the remembrance ;
It harrows me too deeply.

DURAZZO.
                    Can you queftion,
I wifh to fee her unavailing forrow
Chang'd to gay feftivals, and bridal joy ?
Or think you, that fupinely I can view
(Thus childlefs, but in her,) my houfe's honours,
My large eftates, funk in a virgin's tomb,
Or fcatter'd 'mongft remote and thanklefs kindred ;
                                        When,

When, by alliance with your well-match'd love,
Such near and natural heirs may spring to blefs me?

MENTEVOLE.

Why, grant it all, yet how have I prevail'd?
My prefence fhe endures, for you defir'd it;
Yet, if the only theme can touch me nearly,
But trembles from my tongue, her cheek turns pale;
Her blood runs back, as muftering to her heart,
To fortify the accefs more ftrong againft me.
I pity him, who thinks he has known diftrefs,
And never felt the pang of hopelefs love:
The confummation of all other ills
Is light and trivial to that mifery.

DURAZZO.

Time may do much, nor fhall my aid be wanting.
Urge me no more, nor doubt me. Your kind fifter,
Olympia, the companion fhe holds dear,
May unobferv'd watch every foft approach,
And fteal a lover's image on her fancy.
But lo, fhe comes. Farewel! I go to ferve you.
                                    [*Exit* DURAZZO.

SCENE V.

MENTEVOLE *alone.*

He goes to ferve me! Let his feeble breath
Turn ice to fire, wake in her frozen bofom
Such hot confuming flames as I feel here!
O, I could fluice my veins, mangle this form,
This common form, that wants the power to move her.

SCENE VI.

To him OLYMPIA.

'Tell me, Olympia, are not women woo'd
By conftancy, and deep-protefted oaths?
By living on their fmiles, by nice attentions?
By yielding up our reafon to their humours?
By adoration of their beauty's power?

By fighs, and tears, by flattery, kneeling, fawning?
Tell me how many ways a manly mind
Muft be debas'd, to win a lady's fmile?

OLYMPIA.

That which by bafenefs only can be gain'd,
Were better undefir'd. But fay, good brother,
Why do you queftion with fuch angry hafte,
And what ftrange fury ruffles all your mein?
Give me your hand: it burns. You are not well.
Your mind unquiet fevers thus your blood.

MENTEVOLE.

No, no: a woman's coldnefs. Your fair friend,—
Teach her to fmile, and my diftemper dies.

OLYMPIA.

She has no fenfe of joy: that beauteous flower
Bows its fweet head o'er Claudio's bloody grave.

MENTEVOLE.

Muft that eternal found grate on me ftill!
Haft thou been faithful to me? Haft thou told her,
How thou haft feen thefe lids, even at her name,
Swell with unbidden tides of melting fondnefs?
Whole nights how I have fill'd thy patient ear,
And fhe my only theme? How many times,
When chance has given her beauties to my fight,
Thou haft beheld me, trembling, try to fpeak
And gaze away my meaning?

OLYMPIA.

     Nay, my lord,
Endeavours true as mine difdain fufpicion:
And let me fay, if fhe fhould ne'er confent,—

MENTEVOLE.

How's that? take heed! if fhe fhould ne'er confent?
Put not my life on chilling fuppofition;
Make it the doubt, Olympia, of a moment,
And though thou art my fifter, and a dear one,
By heaven, I almoft think that I fhall hate thee:
For here I fwear, deeply and calmly fwear it,
The hour which fees me defperate of her love,
Shall be my laft. —

        OLYMPIA.

OLYMPIA.

For fhame! be more a man.

MENTEVOLE.

By the great power which gave me fenfe and being,
I'll wreft from fate my folly's chaftifement,
And this right hand fhall end me.

OLYMPIA.

Oh! how fhocking,
To hear with what devout impiety,
Thou dar'ft call heaven to witnefs of an oath,
Outrageous to its own blefs'd providence!

MENTEVOLE.

Well, be it as it may, I have fworn it.
Knows fhe that young Marcellus is arrived?

OLYMPIA.

Yes, and the pleafing tidings for a moment
Difpell'd the cloud that dim'd her beauteous eyes.
Inftant fhe beg'd me, and with warmth unufual,
To bear her greetings to his mother Fulvia;
I now was on my way.

MENTEVOLE.

Then, bear thy meffage;
Go, be the agent to deftroy thy brother.
This compliment, I know, is but the prelude,
To invite a fecond Claudio, in Marcellus

OLYMPIA.

If peace be worth a wifh, and love be fuch
In every other bofom, as in thine,
Let the fhort ftory on my grave-ftone tell,
" Nor loving, nor belov'd, Olympia died."

MENTEVOLE.

You never wifh'd more wifely: but forgive me;
Pardon my infirmity, 'tis too like madnefs.

OLYMPIA.

'Tis worfe, for madmen have their intervals;
Thine's an eternal rage.

C

MENTEVOLE.

MENTEVOLE.

Go not in anger :
Return; I will be calm; return, Olympia.
Thus on my knee let me entreat you hear me.
                                    [*offering to kneel.*

OLYMPIA.

'Pray, rise. We may be seen. What is't? go on.

MENTEVOLE.

I have a never-failing instinct here,
Which prompts me what to dread. This young Marcellus—

OLYMPIA.

Well, what of him?

MENTEVOLE.

I know, will see her shortly.
Crowd all thy faculties into thine eye ;
Read his reception keenly; mark *him* too ;
And give me note of every circumstance:
Their words, their looks, let not a glance escape thee,
Promise me so, and from this hour, Olympia,
Thy prudence shall be my sole counsellor:
Though you enjoin me to be blind and mute,
I'll bear it patient as the tutor'd child,
Whose fond instructor smiles, and teaches him.

OLYMPIA.

Keep these conditions, and command my service.
I linger here too long.—Remember patience.
                                    [*Exit* OLYMPIA.

S C E N E   VII.

MENTEVOLE, *alone.*

And what more likely? He is Claudio's brother ;
Noble as he, and deck'd too with the plume
Of brave adventure in the Candian war ;
Younger, and not less comely. She may call it
(As women make shrewd logick for their likings)
'Truth to the memory of her former vows,

I   To

To embrace the living brother for the dead ;
And so find faith in her inconstancy.
I know not why, my genius shrinks at him :
The very *fear* craves vengeance, like a wrong.
Beware. gay stripling ! no degenerate awe
Of what *may* be, can check my fiery course :
She must be mine, and *shall* be.   For the means.
Or good or ill, necessity must shape them.

END OF THE FIRST ACT.

ACT II. SCENE I.

A Chamber in Durazzo's *Palace.*

Julia, *alone at a Table, putting up papers which she
has been reading. She presses them passionately to her
heart, kisses them, and speaks.*

Dear, sad remembrances, my tears have stain'd you.
O, foolish drops, wash not away my treasure!
Unenvied, unobserv'd, and solitary,
Let me indulge this luxury of grief.
My Claudio's soul was pour'd out on these papers;
And every little word recalls him to me,
Lovely, belov'd, in beauty's manly bloom,
Protesting welcome vows, and breathing passion.

SCENE II.

To her Olympia.

Return'd so speedily, my gentle friend?
Your cares are so preventive of my wishes,
I shall begin to expect beyond all bounds,
And grow presuming from too much indulgence.

Olympia.
From Fulvia and her son I bring, my Julia,
A thousand kind endearments. Both together
With cordial acceptation heard your message,
And presently both mean to visit you.

Julia.
Why does not pleasure kindle through my frame,
And mount up to my cheek, at such glad tidings?
The time has been, I should have glow'd at this,
Counting the impatient moments till her coming:—
But my repining heart deserves no blessings.

Olympia.

OLYMPIA.

To labour to forget, I know, is vain;
The fond endeavour toils against itself,
And deeper graves the idea 'twould efface;
Yet there are means————

JULIA.

Unprofitable all.
How have I dragg'd about this weary load,
Through every change of place and circumstance!
I mingled with the young, the gay, the happy;
Forcing a hollow smile at giddy joy,
While my pale heart sat mocking it within:
The arrow sticking here, from scene to scene
You led my sad insensibility,
The objects varying, but my soul the same.

OLYMPIA.

Too much, I fear, we try'd, and you endur'd
Our well-meant, unavailing services.

JULIA.

Could I forbear, I would not weep, Olympia;
Indeed I would not; for it pains my friends.
'Twas such a black, unapprehended horrour,
So sudden, and so dreadfully consummate,
I sometimes for a moment close my eyes,
And strive to think, I've had a hideous dream;
That, still he lives, and I again shall see him:
Ah, no! the short illusion is the dream;
Claudio, thy death the dire reality.

OLYMPIA.

The volume of his days too soon was clos'd;
But grace and honour had so fill'd the record,
Each page out-weigh'd a long life's history.

JULIA.

This was the hour, when my dear father came,
Trembling and pale, to falter out the tidings.
That instant, mighty ruler of our fates!
Had thy exterminating arm reach'd here,
These floods of bitter tears, this black despair,
Had not been number'd with the sins of Julia.

OLYMPIA.

Tame languid minds, whose course glides dully on,
Yield, as the stream to the sharp severing keel,
To close as quickly on each transient wound ;
But woe's deep traces never leave thy breast.

JULIA.

Was I not mad, Olympia ? I remember,
I felt the stab in Genoa.——When I wak'd,
The place, nor aught around me, were the same :
I saw the smooth Bisagnio, as I lay,
Rolling his quiet tide beneath my window ;
It seem'd Elysium, and the peaceful shades
Where guiltless lovers are no more divided.

OLYMPIA.

But now, my friend, col'ect your fortitude ;
Nor start, when you behold your Claudio's image
Recall'd to life, and blooming in Marcellus :
I know, he'll soon be here.

JULIA.

   Why should I dread it ?
Disus'd even to the shadow of a joy,
My sickly apprehension plays the coward :
Yet I will see him.

OLYMPIA.

   You turn pale, my Julia ;
Shall I forbid his coming ?

JULIA.

  No.   This weakness
Will pass away.   A treacherous hectick wastes me :
I shall not suffer long.——Is he so like,
So very like his brother ?

OLYMPIA.

   Features, stature,
Almost the same.   Somewhat a bolder air,
Yet gentle still ; and (youthful as he is)
A little frown of discontented thought
Casts o'er his brow a momentary shade,
That seems not native to his generous aspect.

       JULIA.

JULIA.

In such an aspect was my paradise.
But now pale lead lies on that mouldering face:
Whose beams shot rapture once to Julia's bosom.

OLYMPIA.

By nature fram'd for every genial bliss,
Turn, gently turn, from that cold retrospect !
And there is one ———

JULIA.

I know whom you would name.

OLYMPIA.

Then smile, and name him for me.

JULIA.

No, I cannot ;
I cannot smile, and name Mentevole :
But yet, I much respect him.

OLYMPIA.

Bare respect

For passion such as his !

JULIA.

Olympia, spare me ;
In this alone I must seem obstinate.

OLYMPIA.

Alas, poor brother !   [aside.

JULIA.

Hark ! my father comes ;
Hold him a little moment in discourse ;
I would not have him see I had been weeping.

[JULIA retires a little.

SCENE III.

To JULIA and OLYMPIA, DURAZZO.

DURAZZO.

I come, Olympia, to this chamber door,
To learn my destiny.   As we inquire
From those who wake us, if the sun looks bright,

Or

Or clouds obfure him, and then fuit our garments
To meet the changeful temper of the fky,
So, by the colour of my daughter's health,
My mind is drefs'd for gladnefs or dejection.

OLYMPIA.

I think, fhe mends.   Her forrow, that was filent,
Finds fome relief in utterance.   She approaches.

JULIA.

Your blefling, fir !

DURAZZO.

            O, may it drop upon thee,
Refrefhing as mild dews on vernal flowers,
To kill the canker that confumes thy fragrance !

JULIA.

My heart, my grateful heart, owns all your goodnefs ;
And could my firft devotion reach the fky,
Time and your honour'd days fhould end together.

DURAZZO.

Not too long life, pray not for curfes on me !
Helplefs, uncomely, loath'd, and burdenfome,
I would not cling to the laft hold of nature,
Nor lag without one focial cord to aid me.
Surviving my companions of the voyage,
The world to me wou'd feem to me a ruin'd veffel,
A worthlefs wreck, when mann'd alone by ftrangers.
Let my heart burft at once with fome great feeling !
Let me go altogether to my grave,
Not maim'd and piece-meal with infirmity !——
I have liv'd enough, could I but fee thee happy.

JULIA.

That will not be.

DURAZZO.

            I fwear, it muft, it fhall be ;
And come, I have a fuit which you muft grant me.

JULIA.

My deareft father !   [throwing her arms round him.

DURAZ-

DURAZZO.

Change thefe mourning weeds:
For outward figns, though trifles in themfelves,
When the mind's weak, and fpirits delicate:
To fancy, in herfelf too powerful,
Lend their mute aid, and make her workings ftronger.

JULIA.

This habit was beft fuited to my mood,
But fhall no more offend you.

DURAZZO.

Fair Olympia,
I now muft beg your aid. Your conftant brother,
(Nor does proud Genoa boaft a nobler youth,)
With adoration fuch as faints pay heaven,
Devotes his fervice here.

JULIA.

Ah fir, for pity!
I feel myfelf not worthy of his paffion.
My foul is out of tune to flattery:
The fondeft vows that ever lover figh'd,
Might wring my eyes, but never warm my heart.

DURAZZO.

Nay, ftop thefe tears; I'll urge this theme no more.
And fee, an honour'd vifitant approaches;
Receive her not in forrow.

To them FULVIA; MARCELLUS *behind,* JULIA *and*
FULVIA *embrace*

FULVIA.

Lovely Julia,
In this embrace I hop'd to have clafp'd a daughter;
To have call'd thee mine, by an endearing tie,
That yields alone to nature's clofeft bond:
But though that fleet delufive dream is vanifh'd,
With pride I own thy native excellence.
Thefe eager throbbings, while I hold thee thus,
Are ftronger proteftations how I prize thee,
Than all the lavifh praife my tongue could utter.

JULIA.

JULIA.

Here let me grow for ever, none divide us !
Methinks, when these protecting arms enfold me,
Long-vanish'd peace seems to return once more,
And spread her dove like wings again to shield me.

MARCELLUS.

They told me truth, I never saw such beauty,
                    [Aside, looking at JULIA

FULVIA.

Vile slander, on my life, has wrong'd her virtue.—[aside.
Have I not seem'd unkind, so many months
A stranger here, where ever-new delight
Sprung in our paths ; where each returning morn,
Among the happy, found me happiest ?
But O, I fear'd for thee, and for myself ;
Our walks, these chambers, every senseless object,
By known relation to our common loss,
Had conjur'd up to our accustom'd sense
Sad visions of his looks, his gestures, words,
And multiplied the ideas we should banish.

JULIA.

I judg'd it not unkindness, for I know
Your generous nature feels for all who suffer,
And if to have been once supremely bless'd,
To have reach'd the height of every human wish,
Then sudden—but your swelling eyes reproach me.
You own'd him first, before his birth you lov'd him ;
But O, this selfish grief forgets all titles.

FULVIA.

Yet join with me to bless that providence,
Which bending gracious to a parent's prayer,
'Midst all the perils of destructive war,
Preserv'd one pillar of my falling house.
Come near, my son ; and in this fair perfection.
Behold, what next to thee, the world contains
Most precious to thy mother.
    [MARCELLUS who has been behind with DURAZZO,
        advances.

JULIA.

JULIA.
                    Saints and angels!   [*Starting*.
Am I awake, or is this mockery?
O, I could gaze for ever on that face,
Nor wish to rouse me from the dear delusion.
Still let me know him only by my eyes!
O, do not speak, left some unusual found,
An alien to my ear, dissolve this vision,
And tell me thou but wear'st my Claudio's outside!

MARCELLUS.
If it commend me, Madam, to your favour,
I would not change it for the comeliest form
That ever charm'd the eye with fair proportion.
But stop not at the exterior, search me deeply;
For proof, command me instant to your service;
Though peril walk with death in the atchievement,
Swifter than falcons through the trackless air
My eager thoughts shall fly to your obedience.

JULIA.
Take heed, take heed, tempt not the dangerous shore;
Rocks, shelves, and quicksands lurk, I fear, around me;
And let one gallant vessel's shipwreck warn thee,—
Shun the same course, and find a happier fortune.

MARCELLUS,
I fear no shelves, no quicksands, but thy frown.
Aw'd and enraptur'd I behold such beauty;
And while I talk thus, wish to find some language
Fit for a being of a sphere above me.
            [*A Servant enters, and whispers* OLYMPIA.

OLYMPIA.
Julia, a word. Mentevole attends,   [*to* JULIA *aside*.
And asks to be admitted.

JULIA.
                    Now? not now;
Indeed I cannot fee him. Quick, my Olympia,
Prevent his entrance. My poor fluttering heart;
(If suddenly that name is founded to me,)
Beats, like a prison'd bird against its cage,
When some annoying hand is stretch'd to seize it.
                            DURAZZO.

DURAZZO,

Madam, this day which brings you back to us, [*to* FULV.
We should make festival. Your presence here
Has wrought a miracle. I have not seen
A smile of joy enlighten that dear face,
Heaven knows how long, till you brought sunshine with
     you.

FULVIA.

I have upbraidings for my absence, *here* ;
The cause, I'm sure, a false one. In atonement,
Let me observe her with a mother's care.
Invention shall be rack'd to find new means,
To lure her thoughts to sweet serenity.
She shall not see the frequent tears that wear
Their woeful channel down a parent's cheeks ;
And to the brightest source of mortal comfort,
I will commend her, when I kneel to heaven.

DURAZZO.

May plumes of seraphs waft your pious prayers!
The tenderness of women has a charm,
Our rougher natures can attain but rudely.
Your voices are such dulcet instruments,
They steal the listening soul from its affliction,
To wind it gently in the soft enchantment.

FULVIA.

O, may that power be mine ! Observe, my Julia,
My lord commits you to my guardianship ;
Do you confirm the trust ?

JULIA.
                An outcast's fortune
Might pitiless fall on me, could I fail
To bend with reverence for your dear protection.

FULVIA

Come, let us hence ; the air is mild abroad.
Julia, we must not sink, but strive to banish
That restless inbred foe to the afflicted,
Reflection, from our bosoms.

JULIA.

JULIA.
'Would, I could!
But death's long sleep alone can banish him.
[*Exeunt all but* MARCELLUS.

MARCELLUS.
My soul and all its faculties go with her: [*looking after*
Grace, beauty, sweetness, all that captivates, JULIA.
And holds us long in dear delicious bonds,
Indissoluble bonds, for time too strong,
For change, or casualty, are summ'd up there.
Divinity of love, absolute master,
From this white hour, to thy all potent sway
Thus I submit me: hence, all idle thoughts,
I chase you forth. Full-plum'd ambition, glory,
Arms, and the war, farewell! Her brighter image
Claims all my bosom, and disdains a rival.   [*Exit.*

SCENE VI.
A Place before Durazzo's *Palace.*

MENTEVOLE, *with a letter; and a* Servant.
Convey this letter to the lady Fulvia;
Be muffled close, and cloak'd, that none may know you;
Speak not a word, but leave it, and return. [*Exit* Serv.
Pride and suspicion, in her violent temper,
From this short scroll will work rare mischief for me;
One spark will set her passions in a blaze:
A hint to her is proof demonstrative.—
So,—I must bear this too; she will not see me,
Her health is delicate. But young Marcellus,
He fits a lady's chamber at all seasons;
Soft as Favonius,—and a cherub's cheek
Is not so smooth and rosy. Precious minion!
They think me sure a tame enduring slave,
A trampled clod: they shall not find me such.
The scanty drop which once was patience here,
Flames as it flows, and kindles all my nature
To its own element of fire within me.
Ha! he appears. Choke me not, indignation!
Prey inwards! down! while I dissemble calmness.
[MENTEVOLE *retires a little.*
D   SCENE

S C E N E VII.

MARCELLUS *enters, looking back.*

Ay, there's the attraction. Thou unconfcious houfe,
Thy turrets fhould be cafed with beaten gold ;
For thou enfhrin'ft a goddefs.—Can it be ?
Not three years pafs'd, regardlefs of her charms
Day after day I faw her, and forgot them.
Or does the beauty of the full-blown rofe
Surpafs the promife of the opening bud ?
I fure lov'd Claudio well ; no brother's bond
Was truer to a brother ; yet felf ! felf !
This fudden flower now fprings up from his grave,
That in a brother lies a rival buried.

MENTEVOLE. [*advances.*
My lord, well met. You then have feen this wonder.
Has fame exceeded, think you ?

MARCELLUS.
How exceeded ?

MENTEVOLE.
Spoke Julia fairer than your eyes confefs her ?

MARCELLUS.
All eyes, all hearts, with rapture muft confefs her ?

MENTEVOLE.
Then I muft think, you do not mean to pine
In filent adoration ?

MARCELLUS.
What blefs'd ftrain
Can touch that gentle bofom ?

MENTEVOLE.
Take my counfel ;
Devote thy foul to any thing but love ;
Steep thy drench'd fenfes in the mad'ning bowl ;
Heap gold, and hug the mammon for itfelf ;
Set provinces on dice ; o'er the pale lamp
Of fickly fcience wafte thy vigorous youth ;
Rufh to the war, or cheer the deep-tongu'd hound ;
Be thou the proverb'd flave of each, or all ;

They

They shall not be so noxious to thy soul,
As dainty woman's love.

MARCELLUS.
If this be counsel,
It comes with such a harsh and boisterous breath,
I more discern the freedom, than the friendship.

MENTEVOLE.
Falsly our poets deck the barbarous god
With roseat hue, with infants' dimpling smiles,
With wanton curls, and wings of downy gold.——
He dips his darts in poisonous aconite ;
The fiery venom rankles in our veins,
Infuses rage, and murderous cruelty.

MARCELLUS.
The richest juice pour'd in a tainted jar,
Turns to a nauseous and unwholesome draught,
But we condemn the vessel, not the wine ;
So gentle love, lodg'd in a savage breast,
May change his nature to a tyger's fierceness.

MENTEVOLE.
Away with vain disguise ! Mark me, my lord,
I long have lov'd this lady with a passion,
Too quick and jealous, not to find a rival,
Too fierce to brook him. She receives my vows ;
Her father favours them. Wealth, titles, honour,
My rank in the state, and many fair additions
(Surpass'd by none) keep buoyant my full hopes.
If yet your heart's untouched, I ask, entreat it,
(And strangers grant such common courtesies,)
Forbear your visits to her.

MARCELLUS.
Believe this ;
Were there a fasting lion in my path,
I'd rather this good steel here by my side
Should grow one piece with the sheath, or in my grasp
Shrink to a bulrush, but to mock the wielder,
Than feed you with the smallest hope or promise
I meant not to fulfil.

MENTEVOLE.
Then we are foes.
D 2 MARCELLUS.

MARCELLUS.

I'm sorry for't.

MENTEVOLE.

Deadly, irreconcilable.
Two eager racers starting for one goal,
Both cannot win, but shame must find the loser.
You step between me, and the light of heaven,
You strive to rob me of my life's best hope,
(For life without her were my curse, my burden,)
With cruel calmness you pluck out my heart;
Therefore, were the world's bounds more wide and large,
They could not hold us both.

MARCELLUS.

I little thought
To draw my sword against my brother's friend;
And here attest heaven, and my peaceful soul,
You drag this quarrel on me.

MENTEVOLE.

Yonder herd,
Who prying now would interrupt our purpose,
Will two hours hence be hous'd to avoid the sun,
Then riding at his height; at home I'll wait you,
And lead you thence to a sequestered spot,
Fit for the mortal issue of our meeting.

MARCELLUS.

Since you will have it so,—

MENTEVOLE.

The die is cast.
Have I the bulk and sinewy strength of man,
But to sustain a heavier injury?
Let cowards shiver with a smother'd hate,
And fear the evil, valour might avert:
The brave man's sword secures his destiny.

[*Exeunt severally.*

END OF THE SECOND ACT.

ACT

ACT III.   SCENE I.

A Garden, behind Mentevole's *house.*

MENTEVOLE *alone, on a garden seat, looking at a picture.*

And must I be content with thee, poor shadow ?
Yet she's less kind than this her counterfeit,
For this looks pleas'd, and seems to smile upon me.
O, what a form is here ! her polish'd front,
Blue slender veins, winding their silken maze,
Through flesh of living snow.   Young Hebe's hue,
Blushing ambrosial health.   Her plenteous tresses,
Luxuriant beauty ! Those bewitching eyes,
That shot their soft contagion to my soul ;—
But where's their varied sweetness ? Where the fire
To drive men wild with passion to their ruin ?
Where are her gentle words ? the dewy breath
Balming the new-blown roses 'tis exhaled through ?
Thou envious happy lawn, hide those white orbs
That swell beneath thy folds ! O power of beauty,
If thou canst sanctify—By heaven, my sister :—   [*rises.*
Up fair perdition !   [*attempting hastily to put up the pic-*
                         ture, he drops it on the ground.

SCENE II.

To him, OLYMPIA.
                    'Twas not well, Olympia,
To break thus on my privacy.   My orders
Were strictly given that none should now have entrance.

OLYMPIA.
I would not be deny'd ; and when you know
Why I am here, you will have cause to bless,
Not chide me for the intrusion.

MENTEVOLE.
                    Then be quick ;
For other cares and of more serious import,
Will presently demand me.   Speak your purpose.
            D 3   OLYMPIA.

OLYMPIA.

My lips would give my purpofe little grace,
When fhe, who fent me forward but to find you,
Can fpeak it for herfelf. I came with Julia.

MENTEVOLE.

With Julia ? Do not mock me.

OLYMPIA.

　　　　　Turn your eyes —
To yonder cyprefs, fee who there expects you.

MENTEVOLE.

By all my hopes of happinefs 'tis fhe :
Like a defcended angel there fhe ftands.

OLYMPIA.

Herfelf indeed ; then hafte, conduct her hither.
　　　　　　　　　[MENTEVOLE *rufhes out.*

SCENE III.

OLYMPIA *fees, and takes up the picture.*

Ay, as I thought, her picture. On this face
His eyes were fed, when my approach furpris'd him.
Thou fair confumer of his pining foul,
O, thou delicious poifon, for a while,
Though he may grieve, let me withhold thee from him!
With what a blaze of wealth has he adorn'd it !
What gems are here ! I'll leave it in her fight ;
This filent proof fhould more commend his fuit,
Than hot-breath'd vows, whofe common vehemence
Their common violation quickly follows.

SCENE IV.

To OLYMPIA, MENTEVOLE, *leading in* JULIA.

JULIA.

Well may you be furpris'd, nor can you queftion,
When you behold me here, how deep the intereft
That urges me to feek you.

MENTEVOLE.

　　　　　To behold you,
(What e'er the caufe) is fuch excefs of blifs,

　　　　　　　　　　　　　How,

How, how shall I pour out my enraptur'd sense,
How thank this condescension?

JULIA.
Good my lord,
The anxious bosom, ill at ease like mine,
Partakes no raptures. Calmness and attention,
(If I deserve your thanks,) will better thank me.

MENTEVOLE.
Thou soul of all my passions! this fond breast
Is but the obedient instrument, whose chords,
As you think meet, sound high, or sink to silence.

JULIA.
I have heard of your late outrage to Marcellus.

MENTEVOLE.
Has he complain'd, and to a lady's ear?

JULIA.
Wrong not his well-tried courage. No; the attendants
Saw all your furious gestures, heard your challenge;
And for prevention, to Olympia ran,
To alarm us of the danger.

OLYMPIA.
He's conceal'd.
And has been since your parting. That confirms it.

JULIA.
Waste not the precious minutes in denial.

MENTEVOLE.
Fool that I was! no kind concern for me,
The safety of Marcellus, made you seek me.

JULIA.
And I avow the motive. Am I held,
Like those grim idols barbarous nations worship,
By cruel rites to be propitiated?
If love prevail not, dress'd in smiles and softness,
Array'd in blood will the fell monster charm me?
No; if you prize my peace, if you desire
I ever more should name Mentevole,
Or suffer him in thought, but with abhorrence,
Dismiss your causeless hate to Claudio's brother.

MENTEVOLE,

MENTEVOLE.

Let him dismiss his love to Claudio's mistress.

JULIA.

Your own, imaginary, light suggestion.

MENTELOVE.

He boasts it, glories in it. Causeless hate!
Causeless, to hate the envenom'd thing that stings me?
Diseases curdle up his youthful blood,
And mar his specious outside!

JULIA.

Watchful angels,
Keep him in charge, and o'er his gallant head
Spread their protecting wings, to avert thy curses!

MENTEVOLE.

Ha! am I then———

OLYMPIA.

Is this your promis'd patience?

MENTEVOLE.

What can I do?

JULIA.

What reason bids you do.
Not to repent, but to commit a wrong,
Gives shame's true crimson to the ingenuous cheek.
Ask his indulgence, and confess your frenzy.

MENTEVOLE.

The boy may think I fear him.

JULIA.

No, not so.
What generous spirit is not slow to ascribe
Motives to others, which itself would scorn?
Are you alone too mighty to have err'd?
Rather suspect, your pride revolts to own it;
Acknowledge it, and then have cause for pride,
And rise exalted by humility.
Contrition is fair virtue's meek-ey'd sister;
Her drops can wash offence to fleecy white,
Turning our sins to gracious intercessors.
The wisest sometimes may do wrong from passion;

But

But confcious of that wrong, the ruffian only,
By brutal perfeverance, twice does wrong :
Mean pride ! falfe principle ! true honour fcorns them.

MENTEVOLE.

It goes againft my nature's bent.

JULIA.

Indeed !
Then hear me, hear this folemn proteftation :
If you perfift, by that benevolent power,
Whofe bleffed beams avert from violence,
Whofe law forbids it————

MENTEVOLE.

O, enough ; forbear :
Yes, you fhall be obey'd ; I will put on
The meek demeanour of repenting rafhnefs ;
And to the foe I hate, thus bending, cry,
Forgive me, fince you will it. Yet remember,
I thus degrade me in mine own efteem,
Only to rife in yours. Your liberal nature
Will give my free compliance its beft glofs.
It fhews your full dominion o'er my foul,
That joyfully prefers your leaft command,
Even to my honour, which I rifk to obey you.

JULIA.

The act befpeak itfelf. I muft remember,
My peace, or mifery, was in your power :
You chofe the gentler part, and made me happy.

MENTEVOLE.

Tranfporting thought I behold, I fly to meet him.
The hour is come. Marcellus now expects me.
Farewel ! my eyes, at variance with my tongue,
Still gaze, and cannot bear to lofe thy beauties.
                    [*Exit* MENTEVOLE.

SCENE V.

JULIA, OLYMPIA.

OLYMPIA.

Indeed he loves you.

                              JULIA.

JULIA.

'Would to heaven he did not !
It looks, methinks, like hard ingratitude,
To render aught for love, but equal love.
Esteem, the best affection I can offer,
Seems but a dull, unvalued counterpoise,
And pays the glowing ore with worthless lead.
Though all be little, to give all, is bounty.

[*Exeunt.*

SCENE VI.

Enter, on an opposite side, MARCELLUS *and* MENTE-
VOLE.

MARCELLUS.

Enough, my lord.   This fair acknowledgment
Has rais'd your justice high in my esteem.
A soldier's honour can require no more ;
And sure, 'tis better, thus to join our hands,
Than try their strength in rude hostility.

MENTEVOLE.

I was your brother's friend ; and while he liv'd,
Though the same passion that still fires my soul,
Then fiercely burn'd for this enchanting Julia ;
Yet, from respect for his precedent claim,
And to her choice avow'd, within my breast
I kept the painful secret.   He so lov'd me,
The wound he could not heal, I would not shew :
Then sure, full equally, from you, Marcellus,
New to her charms, at least I may expect
A like declining.

MARCELLUS.

Good Mentevole,
Let's find some safer subject.

MENTEVOLE.

No, this only.
I cannot speak, or think, of aught but her :
She is my essence ; feeds, wakes, sleeps, with me:
Is vital to me as the air I breathe.

But

But mark, I am compos'd; no violence
Lives in my thoughts, or shall disgrace my tongue.

MARCELLUS.

Then, left I move your temper, let me leave you.

MENTEVOLE.

No, pr'ythee no, not thus unsatisfied.
I'll not contend, but her transcendent beauty,
Even at first sight, must strike the gazer's eye
With admiration, which might *grow* to love.
But is it possible, *one* interview,
(For you but once have seen her) should so root
Her image in your soul, that all your bliss,
Or future misery, depends on her?

MARCELLUS.

Regard not me, but reason for yourself.
If all your faithful vows, your length of courtship,
Her father's favour, and the nameless aids
Which time and opportunity have furnish'd,
Raise not your hopes above a rival's power;
Say, were it not more wise, and manly too,
To rouse, and shake off such a hard dominion?

MENTEVOLE.

How cold you talk? Good heaven! I might as well
Resolve to change my nature; bid my ear
See for my eye, or turn my blood to milk;
New-stamp my features, and new-mould my limbs;
Make this soft flesh, that yields to every print,
Impassive as thin air; waste time and thought
On any wild impossibility;
As be the thing I am, and cease to love her.

MARCELLUS.

Then take, my lord, your course, while I shall follow
The counsel which I offer. Once rejected,
No more to persecute, where most I love,
I shall retire, and mourn repulse in silence.

MENTEVOLE.

So then, my lord, my suit is persecution?

MARCELLUS.

I faid it not ; but fince you will fearch further,
I've heard almoft as much.

MENTEVOLE.

And who inform'd you ?

MARCELLUS.

A lower tone, perhaps, may meet an anfwer.

MENTEVOLE.

I *will* be anfwered.

MARCELLUS.

Will!—hot man, farewell !   [*going.*

MENTEVOLE.

Come back. I'll anfwer for you. Your own pride ;——

MARCELLUS.

Ha ! have a care !

MENTEVOLE.

Your boyifh vanity ;
Your fond conceit of that impofing form ;——

MARCELLUS.

I'll bear no more ; this infolence and rudenefs
Have rous'd my rage, and thus I anfwer thee.
    [*They fight.* MENTEVOLE *is difarmed.*

MENTEVOLE.

My life is yours. Strike home.   [*fhewing his breaft.*

MARCELLUS.

Take back your fword ;
And when your peevifh fpleen next fwells within you,
Let this deferv'd rebuke fubdue your choler.
        [*Exit* MARCELLUS.

SCENE VII.

MENTEVOLE, *alone.*

He triumphs every way. Vile baffl.d wretch !
Where fhall I hide my ignominious head,
While love, remorfe, and rage, at once o'erwhelm me ?
        [*Exit* MENTEVOLE.
           SCENE

SCENE VIII.

A Chamber in Durazzo's *Palace, with a Toilet, &c.*

OLYMPIA, *with a picture in her hand ;* NERINA
attending.

OLYMPIA.

The danger's pafs'd, and Julia fmiles again.
My brother, thy divining was too true ;
Her fears were not for thee. But now, to try
This new, this laft expedient.—Good Nerina,
Obferve this picture. This day, in his garden,
Mentevole, my enamour'd brother, dropp'd it.
It is the lovely likenefs of thy lady.
I leave it here. Should it efcape Her view,
Find you fome means to bring it to her notice.
If prodigality proclaim a paffion,
The diadems of kings are here outlufter'd.
And yet I fear—The mother of Marcellus :——
Her eye looks cold upon me. I'll not meet her.
   [OLYMPIA *hangs the picture on the frame of* JULIA's
     dreffing-glafs, and exit. NERINA *retires.*

SCENE IX.

FULVIA, *with a paper.*

What can this mean ? They draw me here to infult me.
I afk for this difconfolate, this mourner,
And find her, where ? Why, with a fecond lover,
With young Mentevole. Her panting bofom
Cannot *expect* his vifit, but explores
His chambers fecretly. O my poor fon !
And could not all thy graces, all thy virtues,
One twelvemonth, keep a miftrefs faithful to thee ?
The Indian pile, that, with the bridegroom dead,
In the fame blaze confumes his life-warm bride,

Is wild romance to our Italian ladies.————
Who cheers our inconfolable in private?
Why, the kind fifter of Mentevole.
Then rumour, which I flander'd, told me trnth,
And *this* tells truth. Let me once more perufe it.

[*reads.*

If you refpeƈt the fafety of Marcellus,
Prevent his vifits to Durrazzo's daughter.
A favour'd lover has her plighted faith,
Who will not brook a rival. Truft this warning.
And fee, the fair diffimulation comes,
Again to figh, to flatter—and deceive me.

SCENE X.

To her, JULIA.

JULIA.

Madam, forgive my anxiety: that paper,————
I hope it brought you no diftrefsful tidings.-
When your eye ran it o'er, your colour chang'd,
And a fad prefage inftant feiz'd my heart,
Fearful perhaps from weaknefs, more than reafon.

FULVIA.

I thank you, no; the import is not new;
It tells me, what the world has long believ'd,
That women can diffemble, and are fickle.

JULIA.

But why choofe you for the rude confidence?

FULVIA.

I fear, there was a reafon.

JULIA.

Pardon me;
Perhaps I've been intrufive; for that brow
Seems to reprove me, for a wifh to know,
What you think fit to hide.

FULVIA.

My interefts, madam,
Muft henceforth be confin'd to my own breaft.

I have

I have no funshine there ; and would not cloud
The cheerful profpect of your coming joys
With ill-tim'd forrow.

JULIA.

Have I joys to come ?
To mix my grief with yours ; dejected, loft,
To keep one object in my wounded mind ;
To hold difcourfe with his ideal form ;
To make my prefent nate, my future hope,
Fears, wifhes, prayers, all ftudies of my life,
But flaves to one afflicting memory ;
Thefe are *my* joys, and who fhall envy tbem ?

FULVIA.

Hateful hypocrify ! O ten times devil,   [*afide*
When, to beguile, it wears an angel's outfide !
[*Turning from* Julia, *fhe fees the picture on the table.*
Ha ! can I truft my fight ? What's this before me ?

JULIA.

What's this, indeed ?

FULVIA.

It curdles up my blood
The very fame ; I know thefe precious gems,
Bought with fuch coft : the eaft was ranfack'd for them.
How came it here ?

JULIA.

By all my tears and forrows,
My murder'd Claudio, on the day we loft him,
Wore this around his neck.

FULVIA.

He did, he did.

JULIA.

He fhew'd it to me ; next his heart it hung
That fatal morning.   By what means unknown,
What wond'rous magick I again behold it,
Confounds me with amazement.

NERINA.   [*advancing.*

Madam, hear me.
In part I can explain the myftery.
Olympia, but a little ere you enter'd,

E 2

Thus

Thus plac'd it on the table, bade me mark it,
And should it chance to escape my lady's eye,
Present it to her notice. In his garden,
This morn (she added) Lord Mentevole,
Her brother, dropp'd it. But I know no further.

F U L V I A.
Dropp'd by Mentevole! his sister said so?

N E R I N A.
Madam, she did.

F U L V I A.   [*To* JULIA.
Ha! did you hear that tale?

J U L I A.
Eternal providence! 'twill then be found;
The hellish deed be traced to its dark source.
O true-divining instinct! now I know,
Why, at his sight, oppress'd with chilling horrour,
Cold tremors crept through all my shivering frame;
Why faithful nature, shrinking, felt the alarm,
As if some fatal deadly thing approach'd me.
Haste, madam, haste! that clue shall be our guide.
Yes, I shall live to see the black detection;
The secret villain's shame, blood shed for blood;
While Claudio's fainted spirit from above
Smiles to applaud, and urge the righteous justice.

F U L V I A.
Can I bear this! Such zeal is worthy of you,
It quite transports you. But first answer me,
How did Mentevole possess this picture?

J U L I A.
O, 'would I knew!—But let us fly this moment.—

F U L V I A.
Did you not *secretly*, this morning, see him?
Answer me quick.

J U L I A.
I did. Of that hereafter.

F U L V I A.
Hold. When a lover has a lady's picture,
A favour'd lover too, though she should swear,

Swear

Swear deeply, till the hoſt of heaven bluſh for her,
She's ignorant how he had it, O, to truſt her,
Aſks ſuch a reach of blind credulity,
As turns belief to folly.

JULIA.
Your fierce looks,
This ſudden anger, are ſo ſtrange to me,
I ſtand like one juſt ſtartled from a dream,
And cannot, dare not think, I wake and hear you.

FULVIA.
Then let me rouſe you from your lethargy.
The flimſy tiſſue of your artifice
Is all unravell'd. By no doubtful proofs
I am confirm'd,—your fondneſs for my ſon,
Your tender care of me, your tears, diſtractions,
Your mourning weeds, (which now, I ſee, are chang'd,)
Ay, and your high-wrought rhapſody this moment,
Were all a publick oſtentatious ſorrow,
Nought but an acted paſſion, a ſtage tranſport;
And I, the fool who pitied you, your ſcorn.
Do you now wake? Now do you underſtand me?

JULIA.
Too well, too well. The peal of dreadful thunder
Will ſound till death in my aſtoniſh'd ears.
O, ſtab me to the heart, daſh me to earth,
And trample my poor body in the duſt;
Try every labour'd, cunning cruelty,
That rage, revenge, or malice, e'er deviſed,
Or was ſuſtain'd by woman's conſtancy;
I'll bear it all,—I would not ſhed one tear;
Would bleſs you, think it mercy, to the pangs
Which wring my ſoul from every word you have utter'd.

FULVIA.
And may the fiend who viſits guilt like thine,
If my reproaches fail, or the world's juſtice,
Supply a ſharper ſcourge, and more afflict thee!

JULIA.
I thought the rigour of my fate accompliſh'd
By Claudio's death; ſecure in one great woe,
Look'd forward with a ſmile to all the ills

E 3   Adverſity's

Adverfity's worft wrath could pour upon me:
But you, inhuman! you have found the way,
To wake fuch new, fuch unimagin'd horrours !—
If there be any power, whofe melting eye
Sheds foft compaffion on us, may that power
Hear, and receive my fervent fupplication ;
Let me be mad, and lofe this fenfe of anguifh !

FULVIA.

What can'ft thou hope from me, but rage and vengeance ?

JULIA.

No, nothing elfe, I have deferv'd them from thee.

FULVIA.

I'll to the duke, the fenate fhall affemble.
When this dumb evidence appears before them,
With all that chance has now reveal'd againft thee,
Think, when thou art fummon'd to their dread tribunal,
Will that fair face of innocence and wonder,
This wringing of thy hands, a few falfe tears,
Shake their ftern juftice ?

JULIA.

O, heaven pardon you !

FULVIA.

If you have prayers, referve them for yourfelf,
Your ftate perhaps may need them.

JULIA.   [kneeling.

Turn, and hear me !

FULVIA.

Kneel not to me.

JULIA.

I kneel not for myfelf.
To thee I am as fpotlefs from offence
As the foft fleep of cradled infancy.
But when your cruelty has broke my heart,
And funk me unrefenting to my grave,
If your miftaken rage gives way to reafon,
(As fure it will,) in that calm, fearching hour,
When you fhall find how forely you have wrong'd me,
Wrong'd her, who lov'd you with a child's affection,
                                        Then

Then cenfure not your rafhnefs too feverely ;
Then try to reconcile your foul to peace,
And O, forgive yourfelf, as I forgive you.

SCENE XI.

To them, DURAZZO.

DURAZZO.

How's this? my daughter kneeling, and in tears !
And anger glowing on the cheek of Fulvia !
Rife, Julia, rife—Madam, that ftern regard—.

JULIA.

O, fir, you muft not pity, nor approach me ;
I dare not truft to nature or affection :
Your breaft perhaps may turn to marble too.
Source of my life ! dear even as thee, my father,
Your Julia lov'd her :—See thefe bitter tears ;
With agonies like thefe am I requited.

DURAZZO.

A fury's brand muft fure have fear'd the breaft,
That could give thee a pang, my joy ! my comfort !—
What have you done ?   [*To* Fulvia.

FULVIA.

                    Do you behold this picture ?
Claudio my fon, the day the affaffin ftabb'd him,
Wore this detefted bawble next his heart.
Mentevole, that weeping lady's lover,
This morning dropp'd it. Afk you, how he had it,
Let that light woman, and her minion, anfwer.

DURAZZO.

And is that fcornful finger for my daughter ?
Injurious as thou art—

JULIA.

                    For pity, hold !
I have enough of mifery already,
Revil'd, upbraided, charg'd with monftrous guilt:
She knew not what fhe faid,—indeed I hope fo ;

                                        But

But let me here fall lifelefs at her feet,
My heaving heart burft with its throbs before her,
Rather than hear your tongue caft back reproach,
To violate the reverence I ftill owe her.

D U R A Z Z O.
Hear'ft thou, inhuman?

F U L V I A.
   Yes, with fcorn I hear her;
That fyren's voice has loft the power to charm.
Why ftay I here to breathe the infectious air?
May curfes reft on thefe devoted walls,
Till livid lightning to the centre fhake them!
       [*Exit* Fulvia.

S C E N E XII.

D U R A Z Z O, *and* J U L I A.

D U R A Z Z O.
Heaven be our guard! What means fhe by that picture,
Mentevole, and thee?

J U L I A.
   I cannot fpeak it.
Pray, lead me hence.

D U R A Z Z O.
   Scarce have I power to aid thee.

J U L I A.
O for a friendly draught of long oblivion,
To freeze up every feeling faculty!
Againft calamity I ftrive in vain;
Since thus each diftant g'eam of flattering hope
Mocks with falfe light, or burfts in ftorms upon me.
       [*Exeunt*

THE END OF THE THIRD ACT.

           A C T

ACT IV. SCENE I.

A Chamber in Durazzo's *Palace.*

DURAZZO, MARCELLUS, *and* CAMILLO.

DURAZZO.

Not fo, not fo; deem me not loft to reafon;
My breaft is ever open to receive you.
Though Fulvia's fon, I hold you not allied
To Fulvia's enmity, and violence.
Nay, were we foes, (which I fhould grieve to think,)
The qualities and virtue of Marcellus
Could find no tongue more prompt in their report,
Than old Durazzo's.

MARCELLUS.

My much honour'd lord,
Thefe friendly founds are cordials to my ear.
Soon as I heard my mother's frantick tale,
(Though tears and exclamations fcarce gave room
For her diftemper'd rage to tell the ftory,)
Such confternation feiz'd me, as if earth
Convuls'd had yawn'd at once beneath my feet,
And livid flames fhot upwards to confume me.

DURAZZO.

Did I not fcorn to mate a woman's malice,
What vengeful fpunge, though fteep'd in Stygian gall,
Could wipe away my deep-dy'd injuries?
My houfe's ancient honour fet at nought;
The little fpark of health, which, juft rekindling,
Glow'd in the cheek of my dear innocent child,
And warm'd her father's hopes, rudely extinguifh'd;
Her name that like a holy word was utter'd,
Grace and good will ftill ufhering the found,
Caft for vile queftion to the public ftreets,
'Midft fcurril cafuifts, and the lees of Genoa :—
By my juft rage, the fanctity of virtue
Never fuftain'd fo grofs a profanation.

MAR-

MARCELLUS.

With burning blushes, as the shame were mine,
And hooting crowds made me derision's scoff,
I own the justice of a father's anger.
Descend, mild patience, to her harrow'd breast !
What fortitude can arm her feeling heart
Against the rankling barb of this fell arrow ?
'Gainst galling taunts, 'gainst mortal accusations,
From lips whose every sound should sooth and bless her ?

DURAZZO.

The malice of a foe may be endur'd ;
But friendship's stab,—the very plank we cling to
Turn'd to a barbarous engine for destruction !—
And yet her gentle, her forgiving nature
Unwillingly permits my just reproach ;
She checks my indignation, by rememb'ring,
How kind, how tender, Fulvia once was to her ;
And how the exalted virtues of her soul
Transcend her frailties, and efface this error.

SCENE II.

Enter an Officer.

OFFICER.

Be on your guard, my lord ; we have certain notice,.
The rabble stir'd up by some strange report,
Mustering from every quarter are assembled,
And threaten insult here.

DURAZZO.

         I thank you, sir.
Let them come on, we are prepar'd to meet them.
The love of tumult, and not zeal for justice,
Is their great principle.   What think you now ?

                      [*Exit* Officer.

MARCELLUS.

The wretch arraign'd, whose gasping expectation
Hangs on the awful pause that dooms or saves him,
Feels peace and bliss to what my breast endures,
Till, prostrate at her feet, I clear my honour,
My reason, and each spark of manhood in me,

                           From

From vile concurrence in this monftrous outrage.
This inftant lead me to her.

CAMILLO.

Hold, Marcellus.
We muft not give too loofe a rein to paffion,
At fuch a trembling crifis. Good my lord, [to Durazzo.
To check the fhameful licence, and difotder,
Which hourly fpread more wide by our inaction,
One way at leaft is plain.

DURAZZO.

My mind's diftracted,
I fhould before have told you our refolves;
But my vex'd fpirit this way finds relief,
And vents itfelf in railing. But 'tis thus.
The duke, (and much I'm bound to thank his grace.)
Though urg'd to every harfh extremity
By that fierce woman, kindly has determin'd
To take the milder courfe. Himfelf in perfon,
When I appoint the hour, will vifit us.
He knows already every circumftance,
In its true ftate, nor heeds our foe's perverfion;
And refting fo, with horrour I muft own,
Sufpicion has its mark.

CAMILLO.
Mentevole.

DURAZZO.

My favour to that lord, his daily boaft,
The prattle of this bufy babbling city,
Pregnant and pofitive in flanderous falfehoods,
The picture dropp'd by him, and found with Julia,
But moft, her fecret meeting him this morning,
(Which, till explain'd, gives colour to fuggeftion,
Have fo perverfely wound us in the fnare;
We ftand, like him, expos'd the common butt
For ev'ry fhaft of venom'd calumny.

MARCELLUS.

Heavens, can it be? That angel! fhe expos'd
To bear the prying eye, the infidious queftion,
Of proud, unfeeling, quaint authority;
Each fauntering varlet, worthlefs of the honour

To

To ſtrew her paths with ruſhes, unabaſh'd
Gaze on the emotions of her lovely face,
And find a heighten'd zeſt in her confuſion!
I will not truſt myſelf to wear my ſword,
Leſt, with a fiery inſtinct, from my ſide
It ſtart at once, and in their blood avenge her.

CAMILLO.

Reaſon and juſtice are her beſt avengers.
Be calm then, good Marcellus: hear the means.
Juſt now, an order iſſued from the ſtate,
That none ſhould paſs the city's ſuburb gates,
Nor veſſel leave the port, till the duke's licence
Permits the uſual egreſs. This, though pointed
But at Mentevole, being general,
Wounds not his pride ; nor can awake ſuſpicion.

DURAZZO.

I fear the wiſe precaution was in vain ;
Suſpicion will awake, when conſcience ſleeps not,
And his—but I am to blame ; appearances
Are indexes full oft which point to error.

CAMILLO.

His ſiſter, as we learn, has ſought a convent,
And will no more be found.

DURAZZO.

                          I pity her,
Poor wretch ! unconſciouſly, the inſtrument
To ſpeed perhaps a brother's infamy :
But all ſhe knew already is divulg'd.
Keep eye, Camillo, on Mentevole.
For you, dear youth, be ſure, no mean miſtruſt
Unworthy my eſteem, and your high honour,
Can ever harbour here.

MARCELLUS.

                          Yet, O, Durazzo,
I feel but half aſſur'd. An ugly ſhame,
Chilling the native freedom of my ſpirit,
Hangs on me, loads me, drags me to the ground.
Nor can i ſhake the vile dejection off,
Till ſweeter than the gale from new-born flowers ;

                                          Her

Her balmy lips breathe peace into my bosom.
Will you not lead me to her ?

DURAZZO.
　　　　　　　　Yes, Marcellus,
Deplore with me the ruins of a mind
Where nature lavish'd every grace and virtue,
To make misfortunes still more eminent.
Come then, let's on.—Without there ? [Enter Serv.] Is
　　　my daughter
Still in her chamber ?

SERVANT.
　　　　　　She but now was seen,
Without attendants, near the orange grove.

DURAZZO.
Ere we return here, should the duke arrive,
You'll find us near the grove. Now I attend you. [to MAR.

SERVANT.
My lord, the stranger we this morn admitted,
Waits in the outward chamber.—If your leisure—

DURAZZO.
I had forgot.　Good man ! yes, bid him enter.
Marcellus, for a moment, pardon me.　　[Exit Serv.
　　　　　　[Exeunt MARCELLUS and CAMILLO.

S C E N E　III.

DURAZZO, alone.
He has known better days ; and, to my thought,
No cares, however near us, can excuse
Our hard neglect of humble misery.

S C E N E　IV.

To DURAZZO, MANOA enters with humility.
MANOA.
I am too bold.

DURAZZO.
　　　　No, worthy Manoa ;
Pride, may intrude, but not the unfortunate.
　　　　　　　F　　　　　　　　　　　　But

But how ? Thy cheeks are pale ; thy ſtartled eye
Looks fearfully around.   What ſudden terrour
Shakes thus thy manhood ?

M A N O A.

O, my gracious lord,
In vain I hoped, your pity and protection
Might be ſtretch'd forth to ſcreen me from my foes.
The cruel vigilance of fate has found me ;
I am diſcover'd, loſt.

D U R A Z Z O.

I truſt, not ſo.

M A N O A.

A dreadful order is but now gone forth,
To cloſe the port up, and the city gates.
It muſt be meant 'gainſt me ; to hem me in,
And yield my life to cruel men who hate me.

D U R A Z Z O.

Diſmiſs that fear, I know the cauſe too well ;
'Tis diſtant far from thee.

M A N O A.

Indeed ?

D U R A Z Z O.

Moſt ſure.

M A N O A.

I breathe again.   May every bleſſing crown you !

D U R A Z Z O.

I know your innocence, and will not fail
To impreſs the duke and ſenate in vour favour.
Nor can I think but for ſome ſpecial end
A providence ſo viſible preſerv'd you.
Mean time, take comfort to you, and reſt here,
Secure ; theſe walls ſhall be your ſanctuary.

M A N O A.

O, ever bounteous to the oppreſs'd and wretched,
The ſtrength of our forefathers be your ſhield !
And, for this manna to my famiſh'd hopes,
When full of age and honours you lie down,
Protect your generation to time's end.   [Exit MANOA.

DURAZZO.

DURAZZO.

Who waits? [*Enter* Serv.] Obferve that ftranger with
    refpect,
And fee that none moleft him. [*Exit* Serv.] O, Men-
    tevole!—
It muft be fo. A thoufand diftant hints,
Like meteors glancing through a dufky fky,
That nothing fhew diftinctly, crofs my brain.
But foon the dim horizon will be clear,
And truth's bright ray difpel the doubtful twilight.
              [*Exit* DURAZZO.

SCENE V.

The Garden of DURAZZO'S *Palace.*

MENTEVOLE, *alone. A whiftle is heard.*

Hark! that's my fignal. Then fhe's near the grove:
And fee, a woman's form. Be firm, my heart!
No fluttering now. Let dire neceffity
(That in itfelf contains all arguments)
Fix its ftrong fiat on my refolution,
And cancel nature's fear. She muft be mine.
I have buffetted beyond the midway flood;
Nor fhall my finews fhrink fo near the fhore.
But come the worft, 'gainft fhame and difappointment,
Thou fharp, but friendly leech, I will apply thee.
    [*He draws a dagger, which he holds up, and returns
        again to his bofom.*
Soft, foft; from hence, unfeen I may obferve her.
              [*retires.*

Enter JULIA.

No, I muft ftill endure; for death is proud,
Owes none obedience; nor will come when fummon'd:
The happy who avoid him, he purfues;
And with malignant triumph loves to enter,
Where dreams of long fecurity and joy
Give ten-fold terrours to the grim intruder.
To thee I ftretch my arms, thee I invoke,
For in thy cold and leaden grafp there—Ha!
    [*feeing* MENTEVOLE, *fhe ftarts.*
F 2   MENTEVOLE.

MENTEVOLE.

Why ftart you, madam? Have a few fhort hours
So chang'd the man you fought, nay, kinder ftill,
With gentle interceffion footh'd, and won
To mercy for a rival, that a ferpent
Rifing on mortal fpires to fting your life,
Could not excite more horrour than his prefence?

JULIA.

Thou art, indeed, a ferpent, coil'd for mifchief;
To dart out on the unwary, drink his blood,
And flink again to thy dark lurking place.
Why art thou here?

MENTEVOLE.

    To talk to thee of love.

JULIA.

Of murder rather.—Hence!   *[going.*

MENTEVOLE.

    I muft detain you.   *[holding her.*
A moment is not long. And can thy wifdom,
For fuch a feather, for one light furmife,
That picture, rafhly deem me capable
Of fhedding human blood, nay, a friend's blood?

JULIA.

Of every crime I deem thee capable:
Thy furious temper knows no facred bond;
Death on thyfelf, even kneeling at my feet,
Thou haft vow'd with frantick oaths. O, patient hea-
    ven!
Why did not fire from yon infulted fky
Confume him quick, ere his pernicious rage
Had plung'd me in this gulph of wretchednefs?

MENTEVOLE.

I am fo clear from any confcious taint,
On that foul charge, I would not wafte a moment
To purge me of fo grofs a villainy.
What ftate, what fex, what excellence of mind,
E'er found an armour againft calumny?
Give the moft monftrous flander but a birth,
Folly fhall own, and malice cherifh it.

                  It

It moves but my contempt.   Confider this,
Art not thou too accus'd ? thy fpotlefs felf,
Alike call'd criminal ? by what ? by madnefs.

JULIA.

I thank thee, yes. Thy moft unwelcome love,
Like fome contagious vapour breath'd upon me,
Has made me loathfome to the public view ;
The perfecution of thy hateful vows,
That firft difturb'd my peace, now blafts my honour.
I ftand a poor, defam'd, fufpected creature :
The eyes, whofe gentle pity balm'd my forrows,
Now turn their beams with indignation on me ;
And thou the caufe of all.

MENTEVOLE.
You hate me then ?

JULIA.

Hate thee ! the term's too weak.   'Tis vital horrour :
The helplefs dove views not the ravening kite,
With fuch inftinctive dread, and detestation.
The principle by which we ftart from death,——
Crave needful food,——nature's original print
To fhun our evil, and purfue our good,
By reafon ftrengthen'd with increafing age,
Are not fo mix'd, and general through my frame.
Hence from my eyes ! Thy fight is deadly to me.

MENTEVOLF.

O, thou unthankful beauty ! think a little,
How envy'd, but for thee, had been my lot :
My youth had glided down life's eafy ftream,
With every fail out-fpread for every pleafure.
But fince the hour I faw thy fatal charms,
My bofom has been he'l.   How I have lov'd,
All my neglected duties of the world,
Friends, parents, intereft, country, all forgotten,
Cry out againft me ; now I count the exchange,
And find all barter'd for thy hate and fcorn.

JULIA.

Dar'ft thou upbraid me, or affume a pride
Even from the homely meannefs of thy foul,

F 3

Thy

Thy long ungenerous importunity ?
Mere sensual love, contented with the outside ?
The pure, exalted, incorporeal flame,
Fann'd not by sympathy's soft breath, expires.
I never gave thee hope, no, not a look,
Thy vanity could construe into kindness.
I play'd no hypocrite ; my heart at once
Diffus'd its honest dictates to my eyes ;
They told thee my aversion, my disdain ;
And were this air the last I should respire,
Here, in the face of heaven, my tongue confirms them.

MENTEVOLE.

O eloquence of hatred ! noble candour !
I am thy fool no more, my doubts are vanish'd.
Thou hast not left in all my swelling veins,
Ore cold compunctious drop, to chill my purpose :
The lover scorn'd, the man now rouses here.
Mark me, ungrateful !

JULIA.
Ha ! what means the traitor ?　　　[*aside.*

MENTEVOLE.

This garden leads to mine ; the passages
Are all secur'd.　A ready priest within
Waits to unite us ; therefore yield at once ;
Vain is resistance.　If I raise my voice,
Four faithful slaves behind yon thicket lodg'd,
Will bear thee off.

JULIA.
Am I betray'd thus vilely ?

MENTEVOLE.

Look round, no aid is near thee.　Thou art mine :
All thy reluctant beauties are my spoil,
And, won by wit, shall be enjoyed at will.
Come ;—nay, no strife.

JULIA.　　　　　　　[*kneeling.*
O, give me instant death !
See, at your feet I fall. .　:.

MENTEVOLE.
For worlds on worlds,

　　　　　　　　　　I would

I would not hurt thy charms. My eyes, my soul,
Are not so dear to me.

                    J U L I A.
            Satiate thy rage ;
With new-invented cruelty deface me ;
I will but smile at the uplifted steel,
And bless you while you kill me.

                    M E N T E V O L E.
                    Have a care !
I mean thee no dishonour; but these struggles,
That heaving bosom, those resistless beams,
Darting their subtile heat through all my frame,
May fire my senses to so wild a tumult,—

                    J U L I A.
O, fatal thought ! I will choak in my breath ;
Fall lifeless here.   Is there no pitying power ?
Are prayers in vain above ?

                    M E N T E V O L E.
                    As empty air.
Love only wakes, for he inspires my ardour.
O, fond reluctance ! must I call for aid ?
No, gently thus— [*stooping to raise her, in the strug-
            gle, the dagger falls from his breast, which she
            seizes instantly, and rises.*

                    J U L I A.
            Ha ! was it sent from heaven ?
Lo, thine own dagger.   See, I grasp it strongly :
Now, monster, I defy thee.

                    M E N T E V O L E.
            Plagues ! confusion !

                    J U L I A.
The righteous guardian of the innocent
Has look'd from yon bright firmament to earth,
And sends this timely succour.

                    M E N T E V O L E.
            Meddling demons,
In black confed'racy combin'd against me,
Turn all my engines to their own destruction.
Yet hear with patience—

                                        J U L I A.

JULIA.
If thou dar'ft approach me,
Stir but thy foot, or call thy bafe affociates,——
Swift as the ray that darts from yonder orb,
(I feel the artery here,) this friendly point
Shall pierce my heart, and, as death's fhades clofe
     round me,
I'll blefs the night which fhuts thee out for ever.

MENTEVOLE.
Obdurate as thou art, alas, my dotage
Would ftill preferve thee ; and implores thee, pardon
The mad attempt by defperation prompted.

JULIA.
Sunk to the loweft in my efteem before,
Lower thou could'ft not fall. Degrading guilt,
How mean, how abject, are the fouls which own thee !
How vile thy thraldom! See the baffled ruffian,
Though bravoes lurk all round to abet his fury,
Abafh'd, and pale, before an injur'd woman.

MENTEVOLE.
I muft endure it all ;—perfidious fortune !

JULIA.
But lo, my father and Marcellus near.
Keep thy dark fecret, for I will not roufe
Their indignation to demand thy life,
And fnatch the forfeit from impending juftice :
Thou fhould'ft not die fo nobly. Hence ! begone !
       [JULIA *throws down the dagger, and exit.*

S C E N E   VI.

MENTEVOLE, *alone.*
Again I grafp thee, faithlefs inftrument !
              [*takes up the dagger*
Revenge, that lateft funfhine of the accurs'd,
If I muft perifh, ftill may gild my downfall.   [*Exit.*

A C T

ACT V.   SCENE I.

A Chamber in Durazzo's *Palace.*

JULIA, *and* MARCELLUS.

MARCELLUS.

'Tis true, too true; my aftonifh'd eyes beheld it.
The duke is come, is in the hall this inftant;
And (fhame to Genoa?) armed guards are pofted,
To fave this palace from the people's outrage.

JULIA.

O, if my prayers have any power to move you,
Or, if you would not add to my diftrefs,
(Moft fure you cannot mean it,) I implore you,
Wide, as if fpotted plagues encompafs'd me
Avoid me, fly me, in fierce Fulvia's prefence.

MARCELLUS.

With joy, in all but this, I would obey you.
Shall I retire, and feem to abet a caufe,
By tame neutrality, and timorous filence,
Which, but to think of, chills my heart's warm blood,
And drives my fober fenfe to wild amazement?

JULIA.

Think then what I feel here! yet, O, remember
She has a parent's claim to your refpect;
And how I lov'd her, heaven that knows can witnefs;
In public to confront her, might enkindle
Her rage to madnefs.   Has fhe not accus'd me
(O, that I could forget it!) of fuch crimes,
As calumny's foul lips might fhrink to utter?

MARCELLUS.

Her's is the fhame, but our's, alas, the anguifh.

JULIA.

Stung thus to frenzy, fhe would hurl on me
Your difobedience; all her houfe's woe
Impute to me alone, unhappy me;

While

While trembling, finking, I could but oppofe
The feeble fhield of innocence and tears.
No, juftice muft for once give way to duty.

MARCELLUS.
O, do not freeze me with fo cold a word ;
Nor wrong the ardours of my glowing bofom.

JULIA.
The great difpofer of events on earth,
For foine unfearchable, myfterious end,
Has pleas'd ro mark me for adverfity :
With conftancy unfhaken, my firm foul
Shall meet the black fucceffion of my fates.
When the full ftorm has emptied all its fury,
This fhatter'd bark may fink at length to peace ;
And the laft wave that rolls the welcome death,
Bury my much-wrong'd name in cold oblivion.

MARCELLUS.
What eye that with delight has gaz'd on beauty ;
What ear that e'er was ravifh'd with fweet founds ;
Who that has fenfe and foul to feel perfection,
And witnefs'd thy unrivall'd excellence ;
Can let thee be forgotten ? Hear, O, hear me !
I can no more fupprefs my burning paffion ;
It will have way   My fate is in thy breath,
And all my enamour'd foul, enflav'd, adores thee.

JULIA.
Marcellus !

MARCELLUS.
Ha ! that cold averted brow,
Prefumptuous man ! befpeaks thy doom too plainly.

JULIA.
Is this an hour for love ?

MARCELLUS.
At every hour,
(Enchanting as thou art) thy eyes command it.
Thus on my knee I feize the bleft occafion,
To tell thee all thy wond'rous charms infpire,
Though ages might glide by, ere half was utter'd.

JUL

JULIA.

There is an aweful witnefs of this fcene,
For ever prefent here, who hovers round me.
Through the ftill void I hear a folemn voice ;
On his pale lips the unwilling accents hang :
Our vows, he cries, were regifter'd above ;
For thee my breaft was pierc'd ; fee this red wound,
Nor lofe the memory in a brother's arms.

MARCELLUS.

What canft thou mean ? Why do thy lovely eyes
Thus wafte their beams on air ? O, turn them here,
To warm my breaft, and light up ecftacy !

JULIA.

May ghaftly fpectres deck my bridal couch,
Hemlock and poifonous weeds be ftrew'd for flowers,
The nuptial torch fcatter defpair and death,
And mutter'd curfes blaft the unhallow'd rite,
If my falfe hand receive another love,
Or my frail heart forget its early paffion !

MARCELLUS.

O, fatal found ! my inaufpicious fighs
Awake no gentle fympathy for me ;
But fan the flame for a dead rival's afhes.

JULIA.

All the moft tender intereft can infpire,
Soft friendfhip, and an anxious fifter's kindnefs,
Unafk'd I offer ; but of love no more :
The object, and the paffion died with him.

MARCELLUS.

Too near, and too remote. It cannot be :
For, O, 'tis lingering torment, hourly death,
To touch the cup might quench our fever's thirft,
And know we muft not tafte it. Angels guard you !
Farewell ! Let chance direct my wandering way ;
The world, without thee, has no choice for me.

[Exit MARCELLUS.

SCENE II.

JULIA, alone.

Moft brave, moft generous, and by me undone !
Judge of the fecret heart, what unknown fin

I   Did

Did I commit, that fate ſtands ready arm'd,
To viſit all whoſe fate is dear to me ?
Take me, O, take me, to thy wiſh'd-for reſt,
And leave mankind to their own deſtiny !   [Exit.

SCENE III.

*A magnificent Hall in Durazzo's Palace. The Duke of
Genoa, with Guards and other Attendants in the
center ; Fulvia, &c. on one ſide ; Durazzo, Camillo, and Julia, with their Attendants, on the
other.*

FULVIA.

I have obey'd the ſummons of your grace,
Yet when I ſee the ſeat of juſtice chang'd
From the grave bench, where once ſhe us'd to frown,
Even to the chambers of my adverſaries,
I look for ſuch an iſſue, as hereafter
Will make this novelty no precedent ;
But to be ſhun'd, and noted for the abuſe.

DUKE.

The ſanctity of juſtice is the heart
Of him who judges ; place makes no diſtinction.
And when the veil of paſſion is remov'd,
When with clear eyes you ſee the good we mean you,
Yourſelf, I know, will thank us for this courſe ;
And own our ſwerving from the common form
Was kind to all concern'd.

FULVIA.
            May it prove ſo !

JULIA.

You ſee me here, brought for ſo ſtrange a cauſe,
I can but with aſtoniſhment look round,
Nor know I whom to oppoſe, or what to anſwer.
'Tis hard to make my affliction my offence ;
And the black deed which ſaddens all my days,—
The ſource, the bitter ſource of every ſorrow,—
The ground to load me with reproach and ſhame.
Yet here am I accus'd,—I cannot ſpeak it,—
Accus'd of what ?—To ſay, I am innocent,

                            Would

Would be such mean, such base indignity
To the great spirit of my exalted love.
I'd rather burst with the proud sense of scorn,
And leave my silence to your worst surmise,
Than utter such a word.

DUKE.
O ! 'tis too much.

DURAZZO.
You are appris'd, my lord, with what intent
My daughter secretly this morning sought
A meeting with Mentevole ?

DUKE.
I know it ;
And grieve to find so gentle an intent
Has met such hard construction from good Fulvia.

FULVIA.
Reserve, my lord, your pity till we ask it,
And counsel ignorance. We know our purpose.

DUKE.
As we our duty. And behold the man
First in our present search.   [takes his seat.

SCENE IV.

Enter MENTEVOLE.

Know you, my lord,
Why we assemble here ?

MENTEVOLE.
Yes. Clamour's throat
Has roar'd it in our streets. I pass'd along
Through files of obloquy. Our sapient rabble
Reverse the order of the magistracy,
And, ere they hear, condemn us.

DUKE.
Then, my lord,
As you regard your honour, and your life,
Touch'd by suspicion to the quick, this instant
Account for your possession of that picture.
That lady there, dead Claudio's mother, swears,

G   It

It was her fon's, and worn around his neck
The day he difappear'd. Behold, do you know it?
Do you allow you dropp'd it?

MENTEVOLE.
Yes; but not
That it was Claudio's. Yet, I cannot wonder,
Two objects fo alike, fhould feem the fame.

FULVIA.
Should *feem* the fame!

DUKE.
Have patience, gentle lady.

MENTEVOLE.
I fay, fhould *feem*; for it is barely feeming.
From that which Claudio own'd (the artift's boaft,)
Myfelf, not meanly in the fcience fkill'd,
Painted this picture; love, my pencil's guide;
And, from the image in my heart engrav'd,
Affifted by the model, fuch I made it,
That not the moft difcerning, niceft eye
From the firft beauteous draught could know that copy.

FULVIA.
And had you fkill to paint thofe jewels too,
Thofe jewels in the round? their hue and luftre
So fingular, and bright? by every power,
Thefe were my fon's.

MENTEVOLE.
No. Give me hearing, madam.
Thofe too I purchas'd from the very merchant
Who furnifh'd Claudio. All who hear me, know
The name of Manoa; his fervices
To this ungrateful ftate; his flight, his death;
Which I lament, fince living, he could witnefs,
And ftrike you dumb, that by my fpecial order
He chofe thefe precious gems, in form and colour
So like to Claudio's, none could mark diftinction.
To pay their value, my eftate was ftrain'd;
But had their eftimation been twice doubled,
A crown imperial deem'd the mighty price,
Rather than yield him preference in aught

Might

Might seem a test of my extravagant love,
I would have grasp'd at it ; and so remain'd
The ruin'd, happy lord of that sole treasure.
Now learn from hence, how wisdom should demur
To found a sentence on appearances.
Your grace is satisfied,   [*Here* Durazzo *whispers*
                                  Camillo, *who goes out.*

D U K E.

                    I own to me,
(No proof appearing to the contrary,)
If this be so, your honour seems acquitted.

F U L V I A.

But not to me. O, undiscerning lord !
Is this your inquisition, this your justice ?
I am not satisfied ; 'my heart still tells me,
That picture was my son's ; so reason tells me ;
Nor should a voucher from the yawning grave
Shake my conviction.—That good Manoa
Did sell these jewels to my slaughter'd son ;
And he, 'tis true, conveniently is dead :
But he had heirs and kindred ; summon them ;
A treasure such as this, could not be sold
Without their knowledge ; instantly convene them,
And act through shame, as if you sought for truth ;
Else, your grave robes will be the jest of boys,
And my son's blood will cry till death against you.

M E N T E V O L E.

Do not suppose I scoff at this grave presence,
When thus I smile in my security.
Produce such witnesses, what could they prove ?
Their ignorance perhaps in what you ask them ;
But we have clear and positive laws to guard us.

J U L I A.

So long I have said little, fearful ever
To give offence, where all my care has been
To manifest respect, esteem, and honour,
Even with a daughter's duteous humbleness.
But thus much let me add : I here disclaim
(As most abhorrent to my thoughts, and nature,)
All common interest, union, and accord,

With

With him, for whom I suffer in the censure
Of that ungentle lady ; and believe,
Firmly, like her, that picture was her son's,
And there, before you, stands his murderer.

MENTEVOLE.

Why stay I here ? My lord, if you have power
To give me reparation for the stain
Cast on my honour by this foolish process,
Pronounce it straight ; if not, thus I withdraw
From those vex'd eyes which gaze with fury on me.

DURAZZO.

Soft you a while ; for lo you, who comes here,
Even to your wish, to make all clear for you.

SCENE V.

Re-enter CAMILLO, *leading in* MANOA.

MENTEVOLE.   [*starting.*

Swallow me, earth ! he lives.   But I must brave it.

DUKE.   [*rising.*

Ha ! can I trust my senses ? Manoa !

DURAZZO.

The same, my lord, and by no miracle.

DUKE.

Yet things so strange are next to miracles,
And his appearance such.   We thought him dead.——
This is beyond your hopes.   [*To* MENTEVOLE

MENTEVOLE.

              O, much beyond them.——
All curses of his nation light upon him !   [*aside.*

JULIA.

The villain's cheek turns pale, his fate has found him.
                                          [*aside.*

DUKE.

Surprise to see you here, no way abates   [*to* MANOA.
Our pleasure at your welfare.   Blushing deeply,
We own the state has wrong'd you, but soon purpose
To give you full redress.

MANOA.

MANOA.
My humbleſt thanks.

DUKE.   *[takes his feat*
At preſent we muſt ſet aſide that care
For one which now employs us.   No more thanks,
We yet deſerve them not.—Come nearer ſtill ;
               [gives MANOA *the picture.*
Take this, examine it.   Do you remember
(Obſerve them well) the jewels round that picture ?

MANOA.
Moſt ſure, my lord ; they are by no means common ;
But all, indeed, moſt rare and ſingular.

DUKE.
They once were yours.   Who was their purchaſer ?

MANOA.
A noble youth, by whoſe untimely death
Genoa has loſt her brighteſt ornament.
Even in the depth of my own myſery,
My heart dropp'd blood to hear the fate of Claudio.

DUKE.
Did you at any time, (think, ere you anſwer,)
Procure for any other purchaſer
Jewels like theſe ?

MANOA.
Never, my Lord.

MENTEVOLE.
               Out, dotard !
Thy miſeries have craz'd thy memory.
To me theſe gems were ſold ; look on me well,
I was the friend of Claudio : think, old man,
A nobler perſon's life, and reputation,
(More dear than life,) hang on the words you utter.

MANOA.
I've ſaid, what I have ſaid ; were my ſoul's fate
Link'd to the teſtimony, thus I ſtake it :
As I do hope forgiveneſs of my ſins,
And peace in death, I never ſold theſe gems,
Nor any like them, ſave to noble Claudio.

G 3

DUKE.

Hear you, my lord?

MENTEVOLE.

            I hear a faithless Jew,
A slave suborn'd, a traitor to the state,
A bankrupt, fugitive, and outcast Hebrew.
Aver—he knows not what;—and still more strange,
I see the credulous duke of Genoa,
The first in estimation as in place,
Gaping to swallow monstrous perjuries.

MANOA.

What interest, lord, have I to do this wrong?
I enter'd, uninstructed of the cause
For which you summon'd me; nor know I now,
Why I am thus revil'd for my true answer.

DUKE.   [to MENTEVOLE.

It can avail you nought, to disallow
The proof yourself appeal'd to.

MANOA.

                Mighty signor,
I have an attestation of my truth,
Beyond all oaths, or sacred form of words.
If I am not a liar, and suborn'd,
There rests within this frame a spring conceal'd
With niceft art, and known to me alone,
And its first master. Touch'd, it will discover
The noble Claudio's image.—Ay, 'tis here.—
Ill-fated youth!—Is this to be a liar?

    [He touches a spring, and shews a picture of CLAUDIO
      beneath that of JULIA.

JULIA.   [eagerly.

Give me that picture. O, my promis'd love,
This was thy form. Thy brow, the throne of honour,
And grace thy minister.—For ever gone!
So look'd those glossy eyes when turn'd on Julia.—
Cold is that tongue.—Come, animating warmth,
Breathe through my lips, give life to this dear shade,
And let me die thus gazing!

MEN-

MENTEVOLE.

Dæmons seize thee !   [*to* MANOA.
Cramps and cold palfies wither thy curs'd hand !
Thou haft undone me.

DUKE.   [*rifing.*

Sir, you are our prifoner ;
And in our palace you muft hear your fentence.—
Bear him away this inftant.

    [*Two of the Guards attempt to feize him.*

MENTEVOLE.

Stand aloof !
Nor raife a hand in violence againft me ;
Or with one ftroke I'll fruftrate all your forms,
And the dark tale dies with me.

DUKE.

Hold ;—let's hear him.

MENTEVOLE.

I did kill Claudio   On the morn you mifs'd him,
We took together our accuftom'd walk ;
When this too certain arm achiev'd the deed,
Which long lay brooding in my jealoufy.

FULVIA.

Deliberate, curs'd affaffin !

JULIA.

O, my heart !

MENTEVOLE.

He talk'd with rapture of the approaching blifs,
Till paffion drown'd his fight ; with eyes upcaft,
Then drew that picture, hanging round his neck,
From underneath his garment ; glew'd his lips
With tranfport, to the beauteous, lifelefs form.
My fmother'd fury rofe at once to madnefs ;
With one hand, from his grafp I tore the picture,
And with the other fmote him to the heart. [JULIA *faints.*

DURAZZO.

My daughter ! ha ! the blood forfakes her cheeks.
My life, my all, look up !

                    FULVIA.

FULVIA. [*running to* JULIA.
Dear, injur'd, maid,
Live but to fee my penitence, my tears!
Thou lovely fufferer, O wake, and hear me!
Alas! fhe heeds me not. My barbarous tongue,
Sharp as the felon's fteel, was fatal to thee.——
See, fhe revives.

DURAZZO.
Thank heaven! fhe breathes again.

JULIA.
O, who has call'd me back to this dark world,
From choirs of angels, and celeftial light,
To view that murderer? Yet, *let* me view him;
For I would find the fpeed.eft way to peace;
And in the hollow of his cruel eye,
There fhould .be mortal mifchief, freezing terror,
To ftop the tide of nature.——Monfter, think,
Pain, ignominy, death, which wait thee here,
Will have their lengthen'd end, but to confign thee
To ever-during mifery hereafter.

MENTEVOLE.
My fentence here I know: the reft's uncertain.
But leaft of all, fur forcerefs! that tongue
Shou:d aggravate the crime, thofe eyes perfuaded;
Thou, thou, the caufe of all this guilt and ruin.
Why did I kill my friend? Why, but for thee.
Why rifk my foul's perdition? Still for thee.
Why forfeit life and honour? All for thee.
Then where fhould I feek vengeance but from thee?
And thus, infulted love thus bids me take it
[*He ftabs*]JULIA, *and attempts to ftab himfelf, but
is prevented.*

JULIA.
Ha!

DURAZZO.
Seize his arm! O, execrable wretch!
Fly, fly for fuccour! See, fhe bleeds, fhe dies;
The fiend, the inhuman fiend has kill'd my daughter.

DUKE.

DUKE.

Quick, bear him hence ; each hour while he draws
    breath,
All laws divine and human are insulted. .[*Exit* DUKE.

MENTEVOLE.

'Tis done ; I laugh at you.   Your triumph's past.
See there, the last despair of outraged love.
Now plunge me in your dungeons ; tire your code,
To wake new torments for me.   The great spirit
Which dared such deeds, shall brave their penalty.
              [MENTEVOLE *is carried off.*

DURAZZO.

Good heaven, in pity to a father's anguish,
Let me not lose her thus !—my child, my child !

JULIA.

The pain of this deep wound is light, my father ;
But O, to think, that your declining age
Will want the comfort of a daughter's care ;
That cold obedience must discharge the office
Affection made so welcome to your Julia !

DURAZZO.

My heart's best blood ! I shall not long survive thee.

FULVIA.

Hide me, O earth ! I tremble to approach——
Has thy soft generous heart one drop of mercy,
To fall upon a wretch, whose savage fury
Outraged thy virtues, pierc'd thy tender soul,
Mocking thy bitterest pangs ?   O, Julia ! Julia !
                        [*kneeling.*

JULIA.

Rise, madam, rise.   These supplicating hands,
Your streaming eyes, and that respected body,
Thus bow'd with grief, and groveling on the earth,
Are sights unfit for her, whose dying beams
With tender reverence must still behold you.
Alas ! resentment, at this awful moment,
Can find no place in my departing spirit ;
For all will soon be peace.

FULVIA.

          Thou saint-like goodness !
Unmov'd I saw thy tears, saw the sweet blush

Of

Of thy wrong'd innocence.   For pity hate me ;
In life, in death, rife not fo much above me.

JULIA.

Give me your hand ; my laſt tears fall upon it.
As thefe diſſolving drops part from my eyes,
So melts the memory of all paſt unkindneſs.

FULVIA.

O, could they quench my everlaſting ſhame !

MARCELLUS.   [without.

I will not be withheld. [Enters.] O, grief and horrour,
Why, why did I obey ?—thy cruel order
Kept me far off.   My prefence might have faved thee.
The ruthleſs ruffian in my faithful breaſt
Should firſt have drench'd his ſteel.   Thefe fruitleſs tears
Are all I now have left thee.

JULIA.
          Thus 'tis better.
A life of forrow, (fuch alas, was mine)
Is well exchang'd for bleſs'd eternity ;
Thine ſhall be long and happy.

MARCELLUS,
          Never, never:
Infinite woe from this black hour awaits me.
Yet let me print on that pale beauteous hand
One sad adieu.   O, that my foul could paſs thus !
By every facred power that hears, I fwear,
My lips thus hallow'd by this holy kifs,
Shall ne'er again————

JULIA.   [eagerly.
          As you regard my peace,
My laſt, my earneſt prayer, let no raſh vow,
Blaſting the hopes of all your noble race,
Replunge the dagger in my bleeding boſom.

MARCELLUS.

Yet, there are means of death————

FULVIA.
          My beſt Marcellus !

JULIA.   [to FULVIA
I beg you do not leave my poor remains,
But lighten that fad office to my father.

DURAZZO.

DURAZZO.

O, mifery!

JULIA.   [*taking papers from her breaft.*
Thefe papers—pray obferve me——
Bury thefe papers with me. Lay that picture
Clofe to my heart, and let my coffin reft
In the fame tomb which holds my murder'd Claudio;
One love, one death, and the fame fepulchre.
I thank your tender tears.—Fountain of mercy!
Mild peace, and heavenly light, dawn on my fenfe;
My pains grow lefs; this load will foon fall off:
I fhall be happy. Weep not. Mercy! O!   [*Dies.*
[*Curtain falls.*

THE END.

Written by JOHN COURTENAY, Esq.

Spoken by Mrs. SIDDONS.

THOUGH tender sighs breathe in the tragic page,
   What lover now complains—but on the stage?
No suitor now attempts his rival's life,
But lets him take that cordial balm—a wife:
And yet, to prove his pure and constant flame,
Still loves his mistress in the wedded dame;
Still courts his friend, and still devoutly bows
At the fair shrine where first he breath'd his vows.
For love, she knows some gratitude is due,
Searches her heart, and finds there's room for two;
And often sees, her coy reluctance o'er,
Good cause to prize her *caro spose* more.
Thus modish wives, with sentimental spirit,
May go astray, to prove their husbands' merit,—
Or ope the door, in this commodious age,
Without death's aid, to 'scape from wedlock's cage.—
Abjuring rules, that soon will seem romance,
Love's gayer system we import from France;
Rescind politely our old English *duty*,
And take off all restraint from wine and beauty;
While lighter manners cheer our native gloom,
As Spanish wool refines the British loom.
  Had fashion's law of old such influence shed,
The raptur'd Claudio ne'er had timeless bled:
His bliss with joy Mentevole had seen,
And Julia's favourite Cicisbe' had been.
The assiduous lover, and the husband's bland,
Like Brentford's kings, had still walk'd hand in hand;
Together still had shone at Park, and play,
Quaffing the fragrance of the same bouquet.
  Our varlet poet, with licentious speech,
Thus far our injur'd sex has dar'd *impeach*.
The female character thus rudely slurr'd,
'Tis fit, at last, that *I* should have a word.—

EPILOGUE.

First then, without rejoinder or dispute,
This *virtuous* circle might each *charge* refute.
That 'tis a *nuptial age*, I sure may say,
With their own wives when husbands run away.——
But truce with jest. Howe'er the wits may rail,
The cause of truth and virtue must prevail.
Of former times whatever may be told,
We are just as good as e'er they were of old.
Connubial Love here long has fix'd his throne,
And bliss is our's, to foreign climes unknown.
If *now and then* a tripping fair is found,
On Scandal's wing's the buzzing tale flies round;
While blameless *thousands*, in sequester'd life,
Adorn each state, of parent, friend, and wife,
From private cares ne'er wish abroad to roam,
And bless each day the sunshine of their home;
Unnoticed keep their noiseless happy course,
Nor dream of second wedlock or divorce.——
    I see the verdict's ours; you smile applause;
So, with your leave, again I'll plead our cause;
New triumphs nightly o'er this railer gain,
And to the last our female rights' maintain.

FINIS.

PROLOGUE,

Written by EDMOND MALONE, Esq.

And spoken by Mr. KEMBLE.

FROM Thespis' days to this enlighten'd hour,
   The stage has shewn the dire abuse of power;
What mighty mischief from ambition springs;
The fate of heroes, and the fall of kings.
But these high themes, howe'er adorn'd by art,
Have seldom gain'd the passes of the heart:
Calm we behold the pompous mimick woe,
Unmov'd by forrows we can never know.
Far other feelings in the soul arise,
When private griefs arrest our ears and eyes;
When the false friend, and blameless, suffering wife,
Reflect the image of domestic life:
And still more wide the sympathy, more keen,
When to each breast responsive is the scene;
And the fine cords that *every* heart intwine,
Dilated, vibrate with the glowing line.——
Such is the theme, that now demands your ear,
And claims the silent plaudit of a tear.
One tyrant passion all mankind must prove;
The balm or poison of our lives—is *love*.
Love's sovereign sway extends o'er every clime,
Nor owns a limit or of space or time.
For love, the generous fair one hath sustain'd
More poignant ills than ever poet feign'd.
For love, the maid partakes her lover's tomb,
Or pines long life out in sad soothless gloom.
Ne'er shall Oblivion shroud the Grecian wife *,
Who gave her own, to save a husband's life.

* —— Spectant subeuntem fata mariti,
Alcestem. Juv.

With

PROLOGUE.

With her contending, fee our Edward's bride,
Imbibing poifon from his mangled fide.
Nor lefs, though proud of intellectual fway,
Does haughty man the tyrant power obey :
From youth to age by love's wild tempeft toft,
For love, even mighty kingdoms has he loft.
Vain—wealth, and fame, and Fortune's foft'ring care *,
If no fond breaft the fplendid bleffings fhare ;
And, each day's buftling pageantry once paft,
There, only there, his blifs is found at laft.

For woes fictitious oft your tears have flow'd ;
Your cheek for wrongs imaginary glow'd.
To-night our poet means not to affail
Your throbbing bofoms with a fancy'd tale.
Scarce fixty funs their annual courfe have roll'd,
Since all was real that our fcenes unfold.
To touch your breafts with no unpleafing pain,
The Mufe's magick bids it live again :
Bids mingled characters, as once in life,
Refume their functions, and renew their ftrife ;
While pride, revenge, and jealoufy's wild rage,
Roufe all the genius of the impaffion'd ftage.

* " Thou art a flave, whom Fortune's tender arm .
" With favour never clafp'd." *Timon of Athens.*